**WI
KI**

CW01567003

III Publishing

Original Paperback Printing May, 1990

Copyright 1990 by J.G. Eccarius

No part of this book may be reproduced in any form without permission of the publisher, except for "reasonable use" and quotations of brief passages by reviewers.

Since the only good lawyer is a dead lawyer, we will enforce this policy ourselves, if necessary.

III Publishing, P.O. Box 620362, San Diego, CA 92162

TABLE OF CONTENTS

	Author's Introduction	5
1	1381	9
2	THE WHEEL	32
3	CHILDHOOD	48
4	ON THE ROAD	66
5	WAGE SLAVERY	83
6	ROCK & ROLL	99
7	STREET FIGHT	132
8	LOVE	147
9	ANARCHY	172
10	THE FUTURE	179

AUTHOR'S INTRODUCTION

There are several people in the United States who use the name Jack Straw; some are anarchists. This story is based partly on the life of one person; though presented as a novel, the stories are true. Some of the events are taken from the lives of other people, and in many cases I have changed locations and other details to the extent that the product may be fairly considered fiction.

My friend says his name is Jack Straw, but I've talked to his friends and most seem to believe this is a name he has chosen for himself. He has a driver's license to prove that Jack Straw is his real name, but he has a couple of other I.D.'s that say his name is something else, which he uses for employment and other purposes, and he asked me not to reveal those.

Most likely he got the name from one of two sources. The Grateful Dead, the folk/psychedelic band that was a creative musical force in the Haight-Ashbury community of San Francisco in the 1960's, produced a song called "Jack Straw" on their Europe '72 double album. Jack has stated that the Dead are one of his favorite bands, and that he attended one of their concerts in 1973, in which case he almost certainly heard the song. Jack Straw is also the name of a character in the Great Rebellion of 1381 in England. At that time the serfs rebelled, burned their Master's manors, and marched on London. They seized that town, demanding that they be set free and given land. Jack Straw and Watt Tyler are among the names of the movement's reputed spokespeople. The King went to the mob, and, in writing, granted their demands. The peasants then returned to what they thought were now their farms. The King and nobles then formed an army, killed those rebel leaders they could identify, and caused the peasants to be returned to serfdom. For those not familiar with this important bit of Anglo history, the story is retold as the first chapter of this book.

Given Jack's interest in politics and knowledge of history, this is the probable derivation of his name; possibly he chose it for its dual derivation. Finally, Jack Straw is about as simple of a name as one can choose in Anglo Saxon. Jack, often thought of as a dual of John, is really a generic term for a man; a straw man, in Taoism and Buddhism, is one who can be cast away, a scarecrow, if you will.

However, Jack claims this is his birth name. His father, he claims, was John Straw, the son of a Knoxville, Tennessee machinist who joined the Marines towards the end of the Great Depression, fought in the Pacific during World War II, and married Juanita Sanchez MacIntosh in time to allow Jack to be born on either the day Albert Einstein died or the night the first Hydrogen Bomb was exploded, depending on which I.D. he is attempting to cover for.

Considering that two of Jack's friends from Seattle say he claimed in that city never to have been to college, it is possible that he did not attend Misketonic University (which is, as everybody knows, Brown University, Misketonic being the Indian name of the burial ground over which the original college grounds were built). However, Jack explained to me that at that time he wanted to organize among the working class, and found his college background embarrassing. I have knowledge that most of the recent events he reported to me are true, so if he fudged in what he said about the more distant past, the reader can assume that his story, as I have written it, at least has some relation to the facts.

In response to some of the critics of my first novel, (THE LAST DAYS OF CHRIST THE VAMPIRE), I have written (in Fifth Estate) that an anarchist novel should have no one hero or narrator. So I suppose this novel is not an anarchist novel, but a bourgeois one about anarchists. But I felt it was important to follow one person's personal development from a severely damaged product of capitalism, the nuclear family, patriarchy, and religion, to being a relatively whole human being. It is a process which every institution in our society is designed to prevent, so if you are on that path, good luck to you.

A NOTE FROM III PUBLISHING

Except for running their works through a spelling checker (which we regret, because English is spelled in such an inconsistent manner) and eliminating obvious mistakes, we do not edit authors' manuscripts before publishing. Who are we to pretend that we write better than the authors? (And editing in any society is not an attempt to prove the literature, but to improve it's marketability or minimize the damage it does to the establishment.) As a result, our end product is not the polished plasticware that is mass produced by the mega-publishers. It is also uncensored. It is organic: from the world of the living, not the world of the dead.

Chapter 1

1381

There were about 80 inhabitants in the village, but if you had asked one, the answer would mostly be "several dozens." The cottages were made of wooden sticks stuck in the ground and thatch, with thatched roofs, and had only two openings, the door and the hole in the roof that allowed smoke to escape. The streets were scarcely more than paths and formed a Y. The main trail led to London after going by the Lord's manor an hour's walk to the west, and the branch went to the village of Blackhearth near the sea. These trails were mud except those few times in the year when they dried to dust. The houses were not so much lining the roads as they were scattered about its vicinity.

The main occupation of the villagers was farming. There was a blacksmith, David Smith, and the midwife, grandmother Jones, and a leather worker, Tom Carter, but they all farmed, just as those who were farmers worked other crafts. The women worked the fields as well as the men, and were held in high esteem by most of the men. They were all serfs of Sir Delraux, who was a knight rather than a great lord. He in turn was vassal to the Earl of Essex.

Jack and Mary Straw had sown barley that spring, as had most of the other villagers, though some had sown rye, and some wheat for the master's bread. Jack had also been forced to work two weeks in Lord Delraux's field, which had made him angry. He was eighteen, so he remembered the time before the latest passing of the Black Death when the Lord had been able to hire laborers rather than use the right of villeinage. The village elders, some of whom were almost fifty years old, said the Black Death had come twice in their lives, that the village had once cultivated much more land for the Lord, and he had lived on the rents. Now there were few people left, and the lord lived well only by asserting his ancient rights.

Where had they gotten those rights? Jack was thinking, because that day the tax collectors would come. In was June, and it would have been an easy day in any case, the crop being planted and the harvest being much in the future. Yesterday he had tended his crop and gone in the fallow lands to gather greens and roots. Today he would pay his taxes, or perhaps not.

They could kill the tax collectors easily enough, but then the Lord and his well armored friends would come, and soldiers they could not fight. "Where was the gentleman, when Adam delved and Eve span?" God had not given the lords the right to collect rents or taxes, they had taken it with a sword.

"Good day to you, Jack," said Mary, his wife, joining him. "Look there at Tom Hobson, dressed in rags like a lousy priest. Does he think they won't tax him?"

"How are any of us to pay the tax? Three groats, for lords and slaves alike to pay. And a third of the crop, and four weeks service to the Lord, and a tithe for the fat priests, and a tax on milling and taxes on all that is traded."

"If we do not pay, they will make you a soldier and send you to France."

"Hello John. Ready for the tax collector? Have your three groats?"

"That I do, but it is a sad day. Parliament writ that the Lord shall pay for his serfs, but Delraux curse his name says the law says he must pay only for the penniless, and we are a prosperous lot, he says."

"Where is John Ball when we need him?" said Mary.

"What good is John Ball. He can preach till he dies. If he were speaking God's truth, the lords and priests and bishops and king would have perished in the Great Dying."

"And many of them did. Not nearly enough."

"I remember the last time he came here," said Mary. "He said each of us is equal in Christ, so we have no need of lords or priests. Let each have his own land and reap his own crop, and there will be plenty, he said. A day of reckoning is coming, he said."

"All fine and good, but there is no fighting the Lords. We have not even swords," said Jack.

"We should learn the longbow, like the men of the army. The great victory in France was by freemen carrying longbow. The arrow pierces the armor."

"That I would like to see. But you're right, longbow we could make, but swords would cost a pretty penny even if David could make them."

So Jack and Mary talked to their friends in the village. Everyone was related if they went back a few generations; Mary was the granddaughter of the midwife and the niece of the smithy. Of the 80 villagers, a good two dozen were Straws, two dozen Johnson and Jones, a dozen Carters, a half dozen Hobsons, and a dozen Smiths. A few others had no surnames at all or odd ones they had taken.

It was well into the morning when the collectors came, the taxman himself dressed in black wool pants and coat over a white shirt, and his two assistants, dressed in coarser grey wool shirts and pants dyed blue. The assistants were big men, standing a full five feet nine inches, and all three had short swords.

The taxmen walked slowly and deliberately to the Smithy's. They knew that in small villages the smithy, if there was one, had the greatest stature; if he paid his tax without trouble, the others would pay theirs. The taxman, one Samuel Cooper, was a citizen of London, the son of an importer of cooking oils. His father had seen the opportunity to turn a quick profit by paying a substantial bribe to the Lord of the Treasury for the right to collect the head tax in Essex. The assistants had been soldiers in France; they were simple mercenaries.

"Good morning, villagers. We carry here the writ of the King and Parliament, empowering us to collect the poll tax, 3 groats from every man and woman of the kingdom over the age of fifteen. We have from your lord, Sir Delraux, the names of the villeins here, and the lord will punish by flogging any who fail to pay the tax.

"We will begin with David Jones. Is this your family, man?"

"It is. Here is your six groats, three for me and three for my wife."

"That woman there, is she not your family?" The collector indicated the eldest daughter, Elizabeth.

"She is, she is but fourteen years of age. There is no tax for her."

"She looks like a grown woman to me. Come here, girl."

The girl did not move. Her father took her gently over to the men. The villagers crowded around.

"You can see she is still a child," said David.

"She looks grown to me. The tax must be paid for her."

"I am not fifteen," said the girl.

One of the soldiers slapped her. "You'll speak when spoken to," he said.

"We'll find out if she's a woman easily enough," said the other, and he grabbed her.

She struggled and screamed as the taxman laughed and the first soldier tore at her clothing.

No one noticed the smithy until his hammer struck the head of the soldier who was holding his daughter. It came apart easily as cheese, with a great piece hitting the ground. Before the second soldier could draw his sword the crowd had jumped him and the taxman and their throats were slit.

The act done, the villager's blood went cold. Several puked up their breakfasts. Many were scared. They kept looking at each other at especially at David Smith.

"You'd best go hide, David," said Grandmother Jones. "Hide in the marsh, and we will bring you food. Otherwise you must flee among strangers. It's best to be with your own people."

"It's not just David, its all of us. The Lords, God curse them, will send soldiers and lucky if any man in this village is left to live. This is no ordinary murder. It was the king's representative."

A babble of voices then arose. A minute later John Jones made himself heard by all.

"If we are to be killed, let's die as free men. How did we come to be slaves? It is the work of the devil, and these men lying here are the agents of the devil, just like the lords and priests. Why should we pay the poll tax, who are just slaves? All over England people hate this new tax, and they hate the greed of the church and the lords. Let's be grateful that we are dead men. Let's send messengers to the villagers with the news, and ask them if they would be free. The lords cannot stand against us if all the people proclaim their rights."

"You are crazy, John," said Tom Straw, Jack's father. "We cannot fight soldiers. There have been rebellions before, and the soldiers cut the people down. The other villagers have done nothing, they have nothing to gain by helping us. They are angry at the tax, but not enough to fight. I say we take our chances with the law. They will look for David, and we'll make sure they don't find him."

Jack wanted to speak, but what he had to say would have been an insult to his own father, and he would have his turn to speak later. But he was mistaken: the rules had changed from the hour before.

"I am going to my brother in village yonder, to tell him what has happened," said Ann, the wife of Simon and a much respected woman. "My brother will fight if you will fight. Aye, I'll fight if my brother will fight."

Without waiting for the approval of even her husband she set off down the road.

Some of the men were more shocked at her presumption than they had been at the killing. Many watched Simon to see what he would do.

Simon watched until his wife was out of sight. "She's a good woman," he said. "I'll take the pence of village yon" (indicating the village in the opposite direction) "and return them and call them to arms. Tom Jackson was a piker in France."

This time the men agreed to it, though a good many dissented.

For a good time the men and women argued what to do. Some wanted to kill Sir Delraux and then live as freemen. Others argued that they would be left alone only if the serfs rebelled in all of England; otherwise the lords would raise an army and subdue any rebellious villages. Some wanted to petition the king to abolish the taxes in kind and make all of them free.

Finally Jack had his turn to speak.

"Soon the word of the fight will reach the lord, just as it reaches our friends. We have to either hide in the marsh or fight. The other villages will not join us if we stand here. Let's get together what weapons we have and march around Essex, gathering up an army. Then we will march on London. The king will have no choice but to give us freedom if we beat his soldiers. We must make long bows and learn to use them."

They did not argue much longer. Within the hour they were assembled with what weapons they had, mostly knives and scythes and a few bows and arrows suited more for hunting rabbits than for killing men. Neither of the messengers had returned. Leaving about two dozen people behind, children and elders mostly, they set off on the branch trail towards the sea. By circling around they could stop in a number of villages and then be ready to attack the Delraux manor.

Jack carried his scythe, his knife, and a blanket; Mary carried the kitchen knife and a cooking pot filled with porridge, a small sack of barley and a blanket. The villages were close together, and in each one the same thing happened: there was a brief discussion and then a good number of the villeins joined the band. By sunset they had reached the eighth village and numbered between three and four hundred.

Jack had never been to most of the villages. Twice he had been to the Manor. Now he and Mary and everyone talked of London, which had so many people they could not be counted. Meanwhile a great feast was prepared, a slaughter of many animals, whose flesh would normally be consumed by the lords or the rich townspeople. Doubtless had there been enough ale they would have all got drunk, but there was little and it was soon gone. Musicians played and many people danced, and a few of the men had the sense to post guards and arrange for their relief later in the night.

In the morning they had not yet returned as far as Jack's village when Sir Delraux came galloping towards them, with two of his soldiers mounted and armed to either side. Fear gripped Jack and the others in the front, and they stopped their advance. Delraux and the others road into the rebels, trampling several, swinging their swords at the dodging men. Suddenly one man armed with a scythe ran towards Delraux and slashed the horse's rear leg before retreating.

A man with a long pike had made his way to where the horsemen were. They had made the mistake of separating, and the piker approached one soldier, encouraging some men and women armed with knives, pitchforks and scythes to group around him. The soldier tried to charge them, but was warded off by the pike. By now a number of people were playing the game of dodging the swords in order to slash the horses. When the soldier tried to turn on one such woman the piker thrust his weapon into the man's stomach.

The mob had tasted blood but Delraux, fearless, did not try to escape. His horse was soon barely able to stand, and only his armor and agility with the sword protected him from scythes and knives. Jack and the others no longer feared the sword so much, now that it was not combined with the speed of the horse.

Before they could cut him down an arrow was shot into his head from only a few yards away. By then the other soldier had fallen to the knives. A great cheer went up in the cloud.

A few minutes later Jack, like many of the others, was again feeling the sickness of coming down from the excitement high. He had found Mary and John and a few others from his village.

"I'm telling you, we'll need long bows," John was saying. "And we have to learn how to work together. We did fine, but I'm not sure we would have done so well if there had been six of them instead of three."

"Long bows are fine," said the Piker, who had come up to them, "but it takes weeks of practice to learn to shoot accurately. Make yourselves pikes out of wood, the height of two men. If you can, tip them with iron. You place the butt in the ground like so when the knights charge and let them impale themselves. It stops their charges alright. They're more dangerous in groups on the ground, but then you can use the pike like a spear. Like so."

The piker went on to another group. Soon the people held an assembly and decided to march on to the Delraux manor. When they arrived there was no one there to defend it: the rest of the family had fled, and the servants welcomed the rebels. There they heard that much of the area was already in revolt.

The next day the main body of rebels set off for the town of Saxbridge, the largest in the area and a full days march away. A number of men volunteered to take word of the rebellion to the other provinces. Thus Mary and Jack set off for Kent. Many people returned to the villages to take care of the children, crops and animals.

Jack and Mary travelled with Daniel Reed, John Taylor, Elizabeth Bloom, and Peter Black. The plan was for Peter and John to continue on West to Sussex, with the others to split up to travel through Kent. None of them had ever travelled, but on the advice of a tinware trader they took a trail south. They decided they would only tell people what had happened in Essex, and hope that the folk would rebel and converge upon London.

Each village they came to was much the same. Huts of wood sticks and mud, roofs thatched with grass, were occupied by happy people. The Kingdom of God had come. Some had fought with the aristocrats, everyone had heard of the rebellion. Some knew an army had headed for London, but most were content to be free men and women now that the lords were gone. All were happy to feed the travellers and direct them on the best roads south.

They reached the border with Kent during the morning of the second day. A group of armed peasants greeted them. They said the people of Kent were being aroused and an army was forming to march on London. After conferring Peter and John set of for Sussex, even though the peasants thought messengers had already been sent there. Mary, Jack, Daniel and Elizabeth set off for Rooks Castle, where the army of Kent was to gather, in order to tell what had happened in Essex.

They joined two other men, Jack Johnson and Wat Smith, who were ready to set off for Rooks Castle. Jack Johnson carried a pike of ash wood tipped with an iron butcher knife. Wat had a long bow, but he also carried a short bow, which he had hunted with. He said he hoped to practice with the long bow before they reached London, in case they had to fight the lords there.

Neither Jack nor Wat thought there should be women in the war party. But Mary argued with them.

"What, men are to be free but women are to be their vassals? Is that your plan?"

"God has decreed that women are to tend the hearth and raise children. Men are to labor and to fight, when it is necessary. That does not make women our vassals. In fact, a woman's lot is easier."

"Oh, the women in your village do not labor in the fields?"

"Well, they do, but only for the sowing and the harvest, when all hands are needed."

"Only for the sowing and the harvest? And they don't tend the gardens, and patch the houses, and all the women's tasks that men do not do, beside? And God is not defending the lords, who claim their position is ordained by Him. I tell you, women are stronger than men, and if you try to lord it over us, you'll learn a thing or two."

"Who is this woman?" Jack said to Jack. "You are her husband. How do you allow her to speak like that?"

Jack just laughed. "If I ask that no one lords over me, how can I ask to lord over someone else? We had better make Mary and Elizabeth pikes, they'll then show the lords a thing or two."

They roads twisted from village to village, but they reached Rooks Castle by the end of the day. The castle itself was merely a tower a few yards across and three stories high and a stone wall half as high surrounding a yard, a manor house, and a small village. A vast crowd of people were camped outside it; a number beyond Jack's comprehension. At first they simply talked to the first people they came to, telling them what had happened in Essex. Some people did not believe them, claiming the rebellion had begun in Kent, but they were impressed that Jack and Mary stated they saw the very first of it.

They learned that a war council had been elected and allowed themselves to be guided to it. It had not set itself up in the castle, but rather in a large tent. People were coming and going, talking and arguing.

After a time a man dressed in the light armor of piker, complete with a cheap iron helmet, came over to them. He had dark hair and a beard and brown bright eyes and had the demeanor of someone who was friendly but capable.

"I'm Wat Tyler. You are messengers from Essex?"

After a moment of glancing at each other Jack spoke. "We were sent by the army of Essex to tell the people of Kent of the rebellion. The army of Essex plans to march on London on the morrow. They have also sent messengers to the other shires. We hope all the people will march on London, and force the king and parliament to grant us freedom. Many of the lords have already been killed in Essex, and the rest have fled to London. We expect to do battle. That is all."

"What will the men of Essex demand of King Richard?"

"That we be freed. That we pay no rent on the land we work, and that we have no obligation to do work for the lords. That is all."

"This is what we agreed upon last night," said Wat. "Elridge, bring the scroll and read the demands."

A young man with hair shaved from his head like a monk, but dressed as a soldier, brought over a scroll of paper.

"First, that the King and Parliament pardon any acts of violence committed against the lords and tax collectors by the people during the rebellion.

"Second, that no man shall pay rent upon his crops, but that villages may farm their lands in common, or each man will be granted the title to the land he works, according to the wishes of the village."

"Third, that all slaves and indentured servants be set free."

"Fourth, that there be no tax upon commerce between the shires, and that there be no tax on foods or cloth."

"Fifth, that all men and women of age are to have the right to vote for their village mayor and for members of Parliament."

"Sixth, the lands owned by the church are to be given to the villagers and priests, and no man is to hold the rank of Bishop, for all men are equal in the eyes of God."

Mary spoke first. "We had not thought of those things, but they are good things. Of course if we are free we must vote. Otherwise parliament could enslave us again."

"Do you think the people of Essex will agree to these demands?" said Wat.

"We would have made the demands ourselves, if we had time to think of them. But people were happy to be free of the Lords, and wanted to march on London to insure their victory."

"Good. We will send a messenger on horseback to the army of Essex with these demands, and ask them to meet with us outside of London. We will set out tomorrow; with this great number of soldiers it will take two days to reach there, maybe three. If you want to fight I suggest you join with my pikers and bowmen. Most people are fighting with their friends and relatives, but we have formed a group that can deal with the lords in case they have gathered their army together."

Except for Wat Smith, who went to practice his longbow, they spent the day learning to use the pikes. A number of men in their group had fought in France and had metal pikes and even armor like Wat Tyler's. They showed how to place the pikes when knights charged on horseback, and how to use the pikes against armored and unarmored foot soldiers. They showed how to use shields in case their opponents used arrows.

They set out for London the next morning, eating the leftovers from the previous night for breakfast. Wat Tyler's group went first, pikers leading and bow-men following. The road was narrow; the soldiers formed more of a stream than closed ranks. They seldom could march six abreast. Twice scouts reported seeing mounted knights, but the lords fled when they saw the size of the peasant militia. Around noon they came upon a grassy meadow and stopped to rest. Before they started again the pikers practiced forming orderly ranks three deep, in case they were attacked suddenly.

When they passed through villages they were cheered, offered food, and given information about the road ahead and any enemy soldiers that had been about. It seemed, however, that most of the lords had fled to London or into the great castles.

The next day Wat and the Council grew extra cautious. They sent out many scouts, and they sent armies to each flank of the main group, though they knew it would be difficult to march in parallel along the roads. Despite being less than a day's march from London the roads were never wider than a carriage or cart, and they led from village to village, rather than directly towards London. Jack, Mary, and most of the others grew apprehensive: they expected to have to fight experienced, fully armored soldiers in a great battle.

Instead they made sight of the walls of London without incident. It turned out the army of Essex was camped at Blackheath, and so the army of Kent made its way there and camped in sight of the city walls.

Mary and Jack did not go to the council of war that night. They were happy to have the rest. Word went round that there were rebels in the city, that the Lords had no army assembled and most had fled to the north, and that the gates of the city would be opened the next morning by the rebels within. Jack and the others were excited that they could enter the city without battle. They talked too of returning to their farms and raising their crops without paying the hated rents and taxes. Some felt God had finally vindicated his flocks; many wondered why God would change his mind so suddenly after so many centuries.

London was a vast city of some 20,000 inhabitants. Jack could scarcely imagine how men could have built such great walls. He did not realize how tall the walls were until they approached the gates. But since his group was the first to approach, he saw that a fight had broken out at the gate, with soldiers trying to close it and others fighting to keep it open. With the other pikers he broke into an undisciplined run. Within minutes the few soldiers who had resisted had been run through; the rebels were inside the city itself.

They looked to Wat Tyler to see what to do. Townspeople were gathering and cheering. Wat set off, motioning them to follow. Before they had gone fifty yards some townspeople dragged out to men wearing outrageous dress to the advancing soldiers. Jack was near enough to hear the talk:

"What have we here?" said Wat.

"These are attorneys. They are the most evil sort of men, hired by the wealthy to talk in the court. The lords do all sorts of wrong, and these men prattle in court so that no plain man has a chance of winning a suit."

"And why bring them to us? We are not your rulers."

The attorneys, who had silent now said, "Please, sir, we are not lords, we have done no harm, we have merely worked our trade, as honest as coopers or smiths. Spare our lives, we are innocent."

"No one dressed so daintily could be innocent," yelled a woman piker near Jack.

"Do what you want with them," said Wat.

"We have no weapons. You have a sword."

"Then you shall use that."

Now the townspeople looked afraid, for none were sure that the rebels might not be defeated later in the day, and none wanted to actually do the act. The attorneys were now lying face down, pleading for their lives. Jack walked forward, took the sword, swung it over his head, and brought it down on one of them. It struck the shoulder rather than the neck, so Jack raised the sword again, and, more carefully, severed the head.

The crowd cheered. Jack offered the sword to the townspeople, and one accepted it, and with effort chopped off the head of the second attorney.

A soldier declaimed, after the cheering died:

"When adam sowed and eve span
Where was then the Gentleman?
Death to the Lords and gentlemen!"

The crowd echoed the last line in a roar and the procession began, heading through the streets for the gentlemen's districts. On occasion they came across a man or woman of wealth, and they spared none. When they reached the quarter of the rich Wat asked Jack and another man, Hob Carter, to take the pikers around to cut of retreat from the district, while he stayed with the less disciplined rabble to punish their oppressors. Then they would assemble before the tower, where word had it the king was staying.

The streets had the aura of a carnival. People were outside talking, eating, sometimes drinking ale that was looted or given away to prevent looting. Jack and Mary's group was soon cut in half, as men were belayed by women and ale. Twice they came upon attorneys trying to escape through the crowd, and both times they killed the fancy-dressed men without stopping to argue. They came upon a few corpses in the street too, attorneys and lords. They came upon ladies, and after arguing, decided to let them by safely. Though they circled around the fashionable district they found few people fleeing. Instead many of the townspeople were looting the rich houses. Their mission being pointless, they moved towards some great fires in the district. There they rejoined Wat and the others, who claimed they had killed the Archbishop of Canterbury.

Soon they had gathered outside the Tower, a great army of people in simple clothes, many still armed with nothing but knives or sharpened wooden poles. The king sent out a chamberlain to ask the people's demands. They were read, and a parchment given to the chamberlain, and then the army waited.

"I'm worried," said Wat. "Richard could grant our petition, and we would be free, but the lords would still be rich, and the bishops would still be rich, and they might well make us serfs again, by trickery or by arming themselves."

"The whole country is against them, Wat," said a woman who had not bothered to wash the blood from her arms and hands. "I would just as soon kill them, but it the king grants our demands then we can send our people to Parliament, and make laws so that they aren't a danger to us. Without us slaving for them their wealth will be worth little enough."

"He won't grant the petition. If he does, we should stay armed and take what we like," said a man.

They argued and argued, covering all the possibilities. Finally a body of them decided that they should go out to take anything of value they could find in the lord's mansions. They were joined by Mary, Wat, Jack and others who felt they should kill as many of the gentlemen as they could, so as to teach them a lesson and reduce the chance of their forming an army later.

Hours later they began to hear the news: Richard, King of England, had granted them, in writing, a general pardon. He had abolished serfdom, and granted all adult men the vote.

Like magic the peasants had begun returning to the countryside. Many, it is true, joined the great party that London was holding, dancing and drinking with abandon. After a quick conference Wat's group decided they would stay together as an army until it was clear that the Lords were decisively defeated. They would camp outside of London that night. First they gathered in a large field and sent out men to gather what soldiers they could from around the city.

"Look, it's a group of Lords!" someone shouted.

"It's the King. Long live King Richard," shouted another.

Most of the people were in no mood to cheer for the king.

The two groups remained separated by about 50 yards. The king's crier came forward. "Send forth your leader, that the king may talk to him," he cried.

After a time Wat walked out of the group, having first gotten them in battle order. Jack could see him talking with the king, but the words were lost. Then Wat moved towards the king, and a gentleman near the king leapt forward and cut Wat down with a sword.

Jack was stunned. Not a word came from the army. Suddenly, the king was riding towards them, alone. As he came close Jack could see that he looked like a boy.

Jack drew the gentleman's sword he had seized earlier.

"A terrible thing has happened," said the king. "That man, Wat Tyler, came to me to bargain in good faith. He asked that we confiscate the lands of the Church, which I cannot grant. He came towards me, and though he was unarmed, the Lord Mayor slew him, for he thought Wat meant me harm.

"I cannot raise your leader from the dead, but I can offer myself to you in his stead. I have granted all that was asked at the Tower: you are free, and you are pardoned, and you can vote. We are all equal under God. There has been enough killing. Accept me now as your leader, and I swear to God that I will be your servant. You will be my army, and protect my kingdom."

"Long live the king!" someone shouted.

"Long live the king!" many replied.

"We are at your service, your majesty," said another.

"Then let us march in an orderly manner through the city, with me at your head, so that the people may see what a great and wonderful day it is."

And the king turned and started marching. Few hesitated in marching after him. Jack was suspicious, and as they walked he talked quietly to others. They talked of killing the king, but decided to instead see that their army kept intact and made its own decisions.

After going briefly into the city, the king told them they would camp outside the city, and led them out through the gates. They camped in a village square almost a mile from the city, and the king's gentlemen brought him a tent and set it up. Meanwhile the king talked to the commoners, asking their names and what their wants were. As they talked to him their suspicions melted away. The King had proclaimed their freedom, and for many that was more assuring than their own acclamations.

They camped, and that night had a great feast provided by the Court. Even Jack and Mary lost their sullenness. Now they could go home and tend to their land. They assured each other that if the Lords tried to take away their rights all the people would rise up again.

The next day the king left one of his attendants in charge of the people's army. Many went into London to check out its wonders. Many more went back to their villages. Jack and Mary spent the day talking to the others, agreeing to fight if the Lords revoked the charter the king had granted. They decided to return home the next day.

Two weeks had passed and the barley was growing high when the news came that an army of the lords was gathering in London. As the days passed the army was said to grow and grow, until it was greater than the city of London itself. Word came that people had been arrested in London and would be tried and sentenced to the gallows. Then the word came that the King had revoked the charters he had granted, and that an army was marching through Essex, so vast that nothing could stand before it. Jack and the other villagers gathered to fight, but when they sent men to scout with men from the other villages those men came back the next day saying the King's army was so vast that even all the villagers together could not resist it. Many had tried to fire arrows into the soldiers, but the armored nights had chased them down.

The villagers hid their weapons and waited. A detachment of soldiers several hundred strong, led by two dozen mounted, armored knights entered their village the next day. They read a decree proclaiming the end of the rebellion and the restoration of the rights that God had granted his Lords. They offered a reward for anyone who came forth and betrayed the rebellion's leaders. Then they left. Word came that the army, many times larger, had camped at Sir Delraux's.

The next day Jack was in his field when a half dozen horsemen road up and surrounded him. They asked his name, which he gave, and soon foot soldiers arrived and bound his hands. They led him back towards the village and the knights rode away.

Jack did not try to talk to the soldiers. He looked at the fields he had loved and nurtured, and worried that they might arrest his wife. When he entered the village he found all the men were there, hands tied, surrounded by guards. The women were crying or watching silently. A gallows was being erected at the west end of the villages.

"David Smith. Jack Straw. John Carter. James Hobson."

The men answered and were separated out of the crowd and led to an armored knight, with other armed men all around.

"Each of you had been accused of participating in the rebellion, of inciting the people to rebellion, and of murder. What do you have to say in your defense?"

They said nothing.

The knight turned to two men dressed as foot soldiers. "You are the witnesses. Are these the men?"

"They are," said one of the men.

"Then I pronounce each of you guilty and sentence you to death by hanging. Take them away."

Now the men resisted as they were dragged towards the gallows. The women followed them, but the men were kept under guard. Jack could do nothing with his hands tied, but his mind filled with hatred. In a minute they were at the gallows, and the ropes were slipped around their necks.

"We should have killed the king," he screamed.

The murmur of the crowd jumped lower. The hangman finished with the nooses.

"We should have killed the lords and we should have killed the king!" he screamed.

"We should have killed the lords and we . . ."

The rope cut into the words, and the world faded from his view.

"You see a guy hurt, or somebody like Anderson smashed, or you see a cop ride down a Jew girl, an' you think, what the hell's the use of it. An' then you think of the millions starving, and it's all right again. It's worth it." [said Mac].

– John Steinbeck, <u>In Dubious Battle</u>

Chapter 2

THE WHEEL

He was cold and felt quite ill. He had tried to talk the others into taking his place, but no one would go for it. He and the weatherman and the redneck and the teenager were standing in the hard packed snow just a few yards from the coils of razor edged barbed wire that marked the outer limits of the U.S. missile base at Mutlagen, West Germany. They chatted quietly, casually, watching both the green clad German policemen on the other side of the wire and the mass of Turkish immigrants and young german autonomen and greens who were walking along the wire, chanting. It was 1983.

The police line near Jack's group thinned as their commander moved most of them off after the main mass of demonstrators. There were other demonstrators around, but they were quiet and scattered, posing no obvious threat to the precious missiles. They were mostly pacifists. The radicals halted about 100 meters away and were up against the wire and were chanting something in German. Now the police were almost all at that point, determined to prevent a breakthrough.

Jack looked at the American soldiers behind the police. They were dressed in khaki and carried M16 machine guns. The word was that they had orders to shoot any protestors who got past the German police.

"What do you think?" said the weatherman.

"This looks like our best bet. Everyone ready? O.K., lets go."

They walked slowly to the barbed wire. The weatherman was carrying a piece of rug, rolled up. The police and the soldiers near them were watching the melee further along the fence. Jack was worried about the rug: they had never tried it, they were taking someone's word it would work.

The weatherman threw the rug on the coiled NATO wire. Jack started from about five feet away, just enough to get momentum before he stepped onto the rug. His foot sank into it but his body moved forward, his other foot pressed into it and he hit the snow on the other side running. He was past the police in a flash.

One of the American soldiers had his M16 pointed at Jack and yelled "Halt or I'll shoot."

Jack thought he had a dozen radical slogans at his disposal but when he opened his mouth "Go ahead, Motherfucker, shoot me" was what came out. He sprinted past the soldiers, expecting to die.

After a while he looked back and to his surprise no one was following him. He was supposed to be the decoy. They were supposed to chase after him so his friends would have time to get out their German, American, and Soviet flags and burn them. Instead his friends were being tackled by the police. He kept running until he was in the center of the field, and then he stopped.

He could go on to the inner fence, but there was no point in that. He became lost, not in thought, but in the sheer enormity of what lay about him. Nuclear missiles. The end of a beautiful planet.

Two german police and two American soldiers came running towards him. He thought of running, giving them a merry chase, but he was sick and tired. He thought of doing what he had done the day before, helping the fool's momentum to take them sprawling headlong into the ice, but he doubted he could handle four of them at once. He even considered making a run for the outer fence in order to avoid arrest, but that seemed inappropriate.

They tackled him and, though he offered no resistance, beat him with their fists and sticks as they held him on the ground. It hurt but he had on lots of cloths to protect against the cold and beatings and it was a distant hurt. They twisted his arm behind his back: that caused a lively pain. He groaned not because he had to but to let them know they had done what they sought to do. They dragged him so that he could not get his feet on the ground and his twisted arm was agony. It was a long drag measured in pain, not seconds. Finally the pain eased, they put handcuffs on him and he realized they wanted him to get up into a bus. Inside the bus were not only his three friends but a half dozen germans who had jumped over the barbed wire spontaneously when they had the opportunity.

It was the fall of 1983. He wondered if he was about to spend an hour in jail or ten years. Either way the wheel had turned again.

That was a long way from Indianmounds, West Virginia and the summer of 1976.

Jack did not particularly prepare for the confrontation session, he just did some thinking. That was about all he was capable of at that point. It was well into the summer and he and his fellow workers were beginning to feel pressure about getting the new dormitory's floor scaffolding done in time to pour the concrete before all the summer people left. By that point Jack was the only one working on the project with any regularity; Barry, who was in charge, was doing some for-pay siding work because he had run out of money. Jack had gotten the hang of the project, but a lot of the work was hard to do without a helping hand. Also, there were no electric tools, or rather there was no electricity to operate them. He was sawing four inch thick pine sticks with a hand saw, a time and energy consuming process.

Richard Right, alleged zen master and the farm's owner, was not around much. The old faker had surrounded himself with the women up in Wheeling. Supposedly this was because the boys had to raise their sexual energies, whereas, being enlightened, Richard did not. Jack's sexual energy was so high he was just about ready to run down a deer.

Jack chose a very simple topic for the group confrontation session. It was in line with their purpose as monks seeking enlightenment, it was a real problem that could be solved at the farm, and it required a leap of intuition to solve.

It was Jack's turn to be the monitor. Being monitor meant that no one could ask you questions back, also you facilitated the meeting, calling on people, that kind of thing. No one liked confrontation sessions, since the idea was to expose people to themselves, especially their hypocrisy and personal illusions. Though they were one of only two or three breaks in the monotony of the farm's life, generally people avoided them, unless Richard Right was there. If you weren't there when he was present it was an admission to yourself that enlightenment was out of reach, or that the farm was a joke and you should be off pursuing a career, getting laid, and eating decent food.

Jack had made a little fire pit out by the bunkhouse. On rare occasions he would ride with some of the other monks into town and buy groceries, but usually he would just give them a list and some money. They did not have a refrigerator at the old bunk house, so food was flour, corn flour, oatmeal, powdered milk, beans, lentils, rice. A meal was simple: setting few sticks set to burning and then mixing flour, milk and a bit of soda into a lump of dough, heating it in a frying pan and wolfing it down before going to work or to meditate.

He smelled like hell. He took three baths that whole summer, none of them thorough. There was no source of hot water. They had a choice of various ice-cold streams and springs if they wanted to be clean. Jack had adopted an "I don't give a fuck about the illusions of the world" attitude. That was a more appropriate zen way of saying that he did not see the point of taking a bath. He also had a toothache, and that was bad that summer. He had not seen a dentist in three years, and was not going to see one for another three years. That's how far he was from enlightenment. He did not even have the sense to go see a dentist.

Richard Right had told him earlier in the summer about refrigerators that used kerosene for fuel. Despite Jack's scientific and technical training this seemed strange. He was thinking of kerosene as a source of heat, not as a source of energy. But he knew that a refrigerator worked by forcing air (or a gas) into a small space; as a result the heat was concentrated, the temperature rose, and the heat escaped to the outside. Then the gas was allowed to expand again, making it cold and providing the refrigeration. So he was able to reason out that by using the kerosene to run a motor it would run the refrigeration apparatus. There was no need to make a deal with the state to run in electric power lines.

The spring problem worked by analogy. You let some of the water run on downhill and turn a waterwheel. The waterwheel then can run a pump that lifts some of the water back up to the top of the hill.

When the session began Jack gave them the problem. There is a spring in the side of a hill, about halfway down. You want to set up a way to pump it up to the house, but you have no outside source of power. You can't use electricity or wind or solar power, and you can't use your own energy, like with a hand pump, once the pump is set up.

He should have anticipated what would happen, but he did not. There were five minutes of silence, after which he planned to ask each person for the answer. Then he would do some rounds of asking people why they had mental blocks about coming up with the answer. Then they would get into the meat of the matter: controlling the body's energies to channel them into the climb up the mountain to enlightenment.

First he had to spend ten or fifteen minutes explaining the question. He had to practically say you had to use the water power itself in order to clarify what was meant.

There were perhaps eight people there, farm regulars. Whoever the first person Jack asked was said "I don't know." It was easy enough to look around the room and see that only two people thought they had an answer. Jack called on all the people who did not know first. He thought it was interesting that the intellectuals had not figured it, but the two working stiffs had. Then he called on working stiff number 1, Barry. "You use capillary tubes" Barry said.

Jack was so flabbergasted he made the mistake of asking Barry to explain himself. Jack commented that it was a good try but impractical; capillary action can only move water so far against the force of gravity.

He called on working stiff number 2, Michael, who now looked less sure of himself. "I thought of using capillaries too, and I think Barry is right in saying that would work. But you could also do it by running a pipe into the spring so that the water pressure forces it up the hill."

Jack explained that it was a nice try but that the spring came out halfway up the hill because that was as high up as the water pressure would take it.

Jack could not believe that no one got the answer. He should have just told them the answer and then let them discuss it until they understood it, and then confronted them with their rigid thought patterns, but he was feeling pretty ornery about the whole thing. He called for five minutes of silence for them to think about it again.

It was about that time that Jack turned the pervasive cynicism that was the operating mode of the Tits of Transmission Society back upon the society. Just exactly why was he hanging out with half-wits in the middle of nowhere, getting paid nothing to work, driving himself crazy by refusing to masturbate or even think about sex?

Meanwhile despair of reaching enlightenment, which he conceived of as both a state of bliss and some deep, secret knowledge of the human mind, and proof that material reality is an illusion, led him to contemplate the future. He would soon be out of money, and that meant having to get a job, which would be quite difficult in Indianmounds. He had a girlfriend waiting for him and decided he would go live where she was and get a job until he could think of some better plan.

Sometimes the Wheel of Life turns and the smoke screen lifts and you are confronted with overwhelming force. No big deal, you can retreat. Of course if you retreat too often you can end up in the Arctic or grubbing for roots in the sub-Sahara.

You go knocking on doors and they are all locked. Now you know what it is like to be treated like a pariah. You may have a big ego and want to sing the blues. A clubman. But when you get there guards are at the door and the patrons are white.

It could be worse. You could be a hippie in 1974 or Adolph Hitler in 1945. The Russians, who you despised both for their social system and their inferior, half asian genes, are eating up German armies like bratwurst. The secret negotiations with the US and England have broken down completely. Factories are being destroyed and whole cities disappear in flames at night. The Capitalists of America and England have no moral scruples about mass murdering civilian populations. Why should you?

You have ordered the elimination of the Jews and that is proceeding apace, but the thought has begun to bother you that history might misinterpret this.

Or just about anyone in 2020, watching the entire earth turning brown and sandy under a sun unfiltered by the ozone layer, wondering how everyone could have been so stupid.

It gets weirder. Ultrabright glowworms on the screen start taking on a life of their own. Computer boxes commit suicide, jumping off shelves. Massive rehabilitations of the living dead in places called BIBLE LAND and RESURRECTION CITY. Where the devil is he now:

On a plain between two mountain ridges. Snow everywhere: piled high in the mountains, blanketing the plane, swirling in from the sky. Cold creeping into the bones dressed for spring, not winter. New Mexico, 1975, the last days of the Vietnam war, the police in hot pursuit, but a van roles up filled with young Native Americans. They give Jack a lift, talk about the weather; he drinks one of their beers, but has nothing to offer in return. Magically he is soon in a valley, thirty degrees warmer, and the mountains really are purple. Dirt sidewalks, diesel busses, a few more thumbed rides, more snow, purchasing some flour, cornmeal, oatmeal, Crisco, a bottle of nutmeg. In the Wilderness cattails were coming up like asparagus and fry up nice with wild garlic and mountain trout. You could see the trail from the cave, but you couldn't see the cave from the trail. Mice nibbled a hole in his backpack, the stuff bag ripped, his $3 pair of sneakers fell apart, and the turkeys, rumored to be nature's dumbest creatures, make a fool of him when he tried to hunt them. He hadn't even heard of the Tits of Transmission society yet.

The Wheel turned and stopped again and stamped on the metal plates that would hold the iron rails was the name Beth. He thought back to that year, a skinny white girl, the New Riders splitting his head with electric country rock. She was now a reality far away but the nipping bar, a forty pound iron dick used to prop up wooden railroad cross ties to the determination of the pneumatic hammer, was close at hand as was Craig with his doll jokes designed to drive a man right out of any mind he had left.

The Wheel Slowed down and he began to focus on things for longer periods of time. Women, jobs, stories, places. They did not raise him in a pressure cooker for nothing. There is no God and there is no soul, but reality is no illusion. Reality is resilient, creating the same people, creatures, and myths over and over.

Which brought him to Rockschool, the edge peering into the depths of the abyss of eternity. It had a physical location, 666 Delancey Street, Manhattan, U.S.A., third floor, and in 4D it was 1981 for a start. Fanny moved out and on his way up and Jack moved into the loft used to warehouse and distribute thousands of samples of new music for America's hottest dance floors. He had nothing better to do.

Yolo was gay and An Important DJ and sick a lot. Something wrong was his immune system, the doctors didn't know what, they could only treat the symptoms. Eve was still alive then, one eye blue and the other brown, and Sherry was living with Harry. Claude came over to share a pipe on occasion, but mainly it was music people, not musicians, music people.

Iman had an attitude that rivaled Jack's and Snark's. He was famous in small circles, like most people, but it went to his head, the easy women and social responsibility. If Iman bought black rubber boots and wore them to the Mudd Club, in two weeks half the new wave hipsters would be wearing black rubber boots. His wardrobe had to be carefully chosen, and luckily he had little money.

Jack was mainly a parasite on his friend Snark, but then Snark was a parasite in his own right, living off a trust fund. Jack was close to being a human vegetable: he had broken up with Patty a year earlier, was still depressed by that and the absurdity of life, and got three months behind in the rent. It was weird living in absolute poverty, no money in his pockets for anything, with a roommate who could blow ten dollars on lunch. Then again, Jack was behaving like a prince. He was hardly even going through the motions of looking for work.

Finally the day of desperation arrived. Steve had told him about a paralegal temp service called Career Blazers. Jack had his suit, and so what if he did not have money to buy shoes to match. Maybe the inter‐ viewer would not notice his hiking shoes. But he had little hope. Tim arrived at the Rockschool and Jack knew he was doomed. Sure enough, Tim whipped out some cocaine. Believe it or not even Fanny did not do much coke, none of them made that kind of money or hung out with serious yuppies or was worth bribing, at least not back then. So business ground to a halt, at least Snark quit answering the phone, and while they continued to pull new samples out of their sleeves and put them on the phonograph and sometimes not listen to more than the first five seconds of the first song, Tim made out lines on a mirror and they snorted up.

Jack had never liked coke much, and this was only the third time he had done it. It anesthetized his nose as usual and otherwise didn't do anything a strong cup of coffee wouldn't do. Soon enough it was interview time. He walked up to 42nd street, not having a dollar to spare for the subway despite having $20 worth of coke dancing in his blood.

Jack was crashing seriously by the time he had filled out the application. It was a good thing he had a resume with him and could copy off that. A young blonde germanic woman interviewed him. It was all he could do to answer yes, or no, or speak in simple sentences. He was so busy just trying to comprehend her and speak in English he did not have time to convey that he really hated working. To his surprise two days later Career Blazers called him and asked me if he could work. Probably they had a big job to fill and were digging deep into the reserves. That got him his first paralegal job.

French, Fried, Franks and Shriners is one of America's best law firms; ask anyone. Many of the world's largest corporations retained the firm; some two hundred lawyers were kept busy at the top of one of the great office buildings of Manhattan. Jack began by working in a profit center. The temp agency paid him and seven other paralegal temps $5 an hour. They sat at the law firm sorting documents by date and type. The law firm paid the agency $15 an hour for each of them. The law firm in turn billed its client, a fortune 500 corporation, $35 an hour for each of them. So the seven workers were generating the law firm $140 an hour. It's true, a good lawyer could charge that much an hour, even back then, for his time, but to Jack it was an awesome amount of money. To the corporation it was nothing compared to their revenues or losing the lawsuit.

Five dollars an hour back in 1981 in New York City. $200 a week gross if you did not work overtime, but by the time they took out federal income tax, state income tax, city income tax, social security and state disability and unemployment taxes you took home about $120. Anything you bought in the city was subject to an 8% sales tax. Marginally habitable one bed room apartments in the area, forget Manhattan itself, rented for four hundred dollars a month. In other words, by the time the government and landlord got through with you, you could eat brown rice and maybe buy clothes presentable enough to go the office in. Needless to say, at that rate of pay the temps didn't care much if they did a good job. Their purpose was to generate profits, not do work.

So he was stuck living with Snark, which meant living with Rockschool, because no way would he pay even more in rent. At least this hell allowed him to save a hundred dollars or so a month, and sooner or later he would get something better.

It was not exactly the dawn of electric rock, or maybe he was not in the mood. New Wave people wanting to make it or, if they had trust funds, kill time in an ego-stroked fashion. Some of the music he liked and remembered later: the Raybeats, the Cramps, Slow Children, Holly Stanton. People would send them punk stuff too, and he liked that better, raw emotion fringed with waking up in the Reagan Reality. The others at Rockschool did not like Punk. It was working class stuff, not intellectual enough. No money in it either, and the girls were dykes.

Jack had written a novel that no one would publish about acid ideologues who figured out a way to spray LSD into the air and did it in Washington, D.C. Sometimes he would write other things, and he thought a lot about how the mind works and how you could duplicate it with computers. But he was isolated, he did not even go to the library to find out what others were thinking about it. Fortunately Snark was generous with his ganja, and Jack availed myself to that a couple of times a week. Jack had plenty of acid but wisely did not take it: New York City was just too crazy and his mind was wearing too thin to risk it.

As luck would have it he had a friend in Berkeley who would send him crystal methedrine. Evil stuff. A line about an inch long and an eighth of an inch wide has the effect of a cup of strong coffee, only clean. Good if you have to start to work early after a night of partying, or want to finish a short story, or do that night of partying, or write a computer program. It's easy to vary the dose: two inches to go dancing, thicker to write crazy, repeat the dose to feel like a demon. Most people lose control real fast. Lines get to be four inches long and snorted up the nose until either all of the meth or all of the mind is gone. Even beginners can go through a quarter gram in a day or two. Jack was consuming about a tenth of a gram a month, plus tea, plus some coffee. Only constantly reminding himself of seeing people age five years during a single month of abuse kept him from upping the dose. Much.

It was a combination of the noise and being at a loss for what to do that did him in. Jack did not want to be a lawyer and did not have the ambition to find a well paying computer programming job, or to manage a band. He felt a failure as a writer since he could not find a publisher. Delancey Street had six lanes of traffic and Allen street had four: Rockschool was at the corner. Around 3 a.m. when the traffic slowed down you could feel the building shake when the M train went by directly beneath the building. Snark would breeze in around 5 a.m. and watch some TV, winding down before going to bed. The living room was usually piled high with boxes of promotional records that they had to repack and ship out to the supercool D.J.'s around the U.S.

Politics. Skip this if you don't want to hear about it. Jack hated nuclear weapons more than anything. It was hard to be serious about the future in a world with 60,000 nukes. So when he walked by a table in the West Village and saw some sort of sign about civil disobedience against nuclear weapons he took a flier. He went to the civil disobedience training and for the first time encountered non-violent fascism. He was supposed to learn how to be nonviolent. Like American sheep need to learn to be non-violent. They need to learn how to riot. Let the soldiers and bankers take courses in non-violence. But he joined an affinity group with some interesting people in it and he went down to the UN and sat down and they even pulled over a barricade. A big cop swung his club and the other cops actually dragged him back. It was a media event staged by liberals and stalinists, but he was too naive to know that. He was arrested with the others, put on a bus, taken to Brooklyn, given a ticket and released.

Nuclear war was real, it just hadn't happened. Jack volunteered for Mobilization for Survival, novice that he was, and with some other volunteers formed a committee for Direct Action. The Mobe heavies didn't like it so Jack's group split and formed their own group.

But time was running out. He was fired from the paralegal temp service for playing backgammon with his friend Andrew at Divots, Yolks & Warsell. Fascism with a smile. Unemployment was little compensation and would not last long. Snark was situating Rockschool to sell out.

He knew the world was destroying him as surely as it was destroying itself.

He bailed out. He left everything behind, got on a plane, and flew to Seattle.

The Wheel turned.

Chapter 3

CHILDHOOD

Trinity Academy. Fire ants swarming over Randy, screaming. They did not mean to drop him in the nest. Black asphalt parking lot playground. Jeff, the bully, charging at him, Jack reacting unthinking, ducking his head, leaning to the left and letting Jeff crash over his hip to end up lying bleeding on the asphalt. Spankings by Mother: can't you keep from falling? How many knees of pants do I have to patch?

Grey pants, all the same, white shirts, all the same, green ties, all the same, black patent leather shoes, all the same. For the girls, already a separate race, green plaid skirts, white blouses, patent black and white shoes, green socks, and a funny green hat like an inverted rowboat. Still, there are differences. Some are taller, some shorter; some have parents who speak "correctly", others in the common southern slang; some have parents who insist they do their homework. In a city where more than half the people are black skinned the school is all white; the black skinned children all attend St. Paul, at the beach.

By the time Jack made it to Sixth Grade he was a total mess. He had been told so many contradictory things, been spanked for so many different types of behavior, been ostracized by every social group. Going to school was an exercise in defeat. Adolescent hormones were beginning to kick in, but he spent his time wondering why everyone was not Catholic if an all powerful God had chosen Catholicism for his favorite religion. But he was getting good grades in school, which required severe damping of critical facilities.

Even so, he hated Mrs. Lopez. Mrs. Lopez's idea of teaching mathematics was having the classes (she taught the sixth and seventh grades simultaneously) memorize her table of fractions and their percent equivalents. Jack did not see the point. If you want the percent equivalent of a fraction, he had already learned, you just divide the bottom number into the top number. He knew of no easy way to go the opposite way, but he figured out that any decimal could be converted to hundredths, or thousandths, or whatever, and then you could find common numbers that went into the bigger numbers. For instance, .125 is 125 thousandths, so you divide twenty five into both, so its 5, let's see, 40ths, so it's 1/8th. But Mrs. Lopez did not care about that: she gave you a list of fifty conversions and ten minutes to do them: five per minute. Memorization. Jack hated it.

Most of the kids hated Mrs. Lopez. It was hard to explain why her more than most teachers. She just took the life out of everything. If it wasn't dead she did not want to be around it. She said the U.S. should nuke the Soviet Union. One of the kids asked her why. She said because they are atheists and God was sending them to hell anyway. Someone asked how they could be Catholics if their government never let them even know about Christ. She said God appeared to each one of them, and they had rejected them. She was Cuban, a refugee from Castro.

Jack wasn't on particularly bad terms with his classmates that year, but mainly he was shunned for his weakness of character and for setting a bad example the previous two years by getting the best grades in the class. He still got mostly A's, but now his classmates were used to it and a couple of girls with good memories were getting better grades, so he was less of a threat.

Bill Speed was his best friend, though they were not that close, because Bill was an outsider; his parents had just moved to Jacksonville. True to name, Bill could run fast. He was several inches taller than Jack. He had a fraternal twin sister named Sarah who was also in the sixth grade.

When Mrs. Lopez left to exchange classes with Miss Murphy, who came over to teach science, there was often a brief respite of freedom. Mainly people would talk; friends who had been separated to keep them from talking during class would stroll over to their friend's desks. Sometimes games would start, paper football being a favorite. Cooties, a game of tag, was another. Occasionally Miss Murphy would be quite late; she was still in college herself, taking classes. (In Jacksonville in 1967 teachers only needed a high school diploma to teach elementary school.) The same process often happened in reverse: Mrs. Lopez would be late coming back. This was a more dangerous situation: Mrs. Lopez punished people for being away from their desks, whereas Miss Murphy just wanted you to get back to your desk.

The game of Tag had escalated. Sarah was it and Jack and Bill were teasing her when Mrs. Lopez walked in. They got called to the front of the room. "Why were you away from your desks?" she said. "What are you doing running in Church?"

Technically they were not in Church, since the divider was up making the classroom, but this was part of Mrs. Lopez's technique of making the most venial sin seem mortal.

Jack was in a state of total paralysis. He had seldom been punished at school. He knew getting punished at school meant getting triply punished at home. He was not even thinking that clearly: it was just a reaction. None of the children said anything. Mrs. Lopez sent them over to the other building to see the Principal, Mrs. Rich, who was also the first grade teacher. It was embarrassing standing in front of the first graders. Mrs. Rich had been Jack's first grade teacher, and he had liked her O.K. back then. She looked something like his mother: a strong face, brown eyes, black hair. Wasps might think "Spic" but he did not know that then. Just that she wanted to know why they were sent over.

"We were away from our seats between classes," he said.

Mrs. Rich considered them. "I want you to go to the back of the class and sit. You're old enough you should know how to conduct yourselves in a classroom."

There were some chairs in the back of the classroom for when parents or others came into observe. The sat in them, listened to Mrs. Rich for a while, became bored, daydreamed.

Jack imagined the building was surrounded by Clors, a particularly dangerous people in his imaginary world. Their favorite weapon was the spear. Being fair warriors, Jack, his generals Kim and Chris, and their soldiers also fought with spears. Casualties were mounting; a messenger came in saying that the Clors had broken into the fifth grade classroom and there was fighting in the halls. Jack wanted to get up and defend the hallway, but Kim insisted that Jack not get into trouble in the other world, and he went out bravely into the hall to rally the men himself (in his mind).

"Now I'm leaving the classroom for a while," Mrs. Rich said, gaining Jack's attention. "And I want our sixth graders back there to observe that my first graders behave themselves like perfect ladies and gentlemen when I am absent. Now everyone just go ahead and practice your writing while I'm out."

As she walked out Bill whispered "what did you tell her we were away from our desks for?"

"I guess I shouldn't have," said Jack.

Almost as soon as the door closed one of the first graders went to it, opened it carefully, and peered out the crack. "She went into the office" the child said.

A soft roar of voices sprang up. Another child went to the back door and opened it a crack, to prevent a surprise from the rear. Children began drifting around the room. Three girls set up a jump rope and started jumping. One boy stood up on his desk and pretended he was an airplane. Others threw wads of paper at each other. Soon straws were produced and a spitball war broke out. A large group of girls huddled in one corner, talking and laughing. Two girls and a boy started looking at the things inside of Mrs. Rich's desk. The children ignored the sixth-graders, not even bothering to aim spitballs at them.

Five minutes of anarchy passed. No murders occurred. The child at the door said, in a loud panicky whisper, "She's coming."

The jump rope disappeared. The loose paper was snatched up. Silence was broken only by footsteps closing in on desks. By the time Mrs. Rick opened the door all the children were practicing their writing.

Mrs. Rick smiled. She looked at the sixth graders. "Do you think you know how to conduct yourselves now?"

"Yes, Mrs. Rich," they said, almost in unison.

And they were free to return to Mrs. Lopez's kingdom.

The grass of the front yard was green and mowed, so that passing by from a car along the street it looked like perfect sod. But Mrs. Straw insisted upon planting the yard with a variety of grass not suited to the local climate. As a result local grasses and weeds made rapid inroads that no amount of mowing, reseeding, watering, fertilizing, and weeding cured, and there were even small patches of nude soil where weeds had been uprooted but the favored grass had not spread. Because it was Fall, and Fall lasts all winter in Jacksonville, there were leaves scattered about the yard from the evergreen and ever shedding live oak and magnolia trees. Every weekend Mrs. Straw forced her two sons to rake up the leaves, a task that took hours, and by Tuesday if not Monday the lawn is not sufficiently well manicured for her tastes.

The room was perhaps ten feet long and eight feet wide. Over the years the furniture had permuted through a variety of configurations, but the last few years it had been stable, with the beds against the south and the east walls, a chest of drawers between them, the desks against the west wall, with its centered window, and the north wall with a door leading to the closet and a chest of drawers between it and the door leading to the rest of the house. Roughly, Jack occupies the north area of the room and his brother Chris the south.

Jack's area was his sanctuary, but it was not inviolable. It was simply the coolest part of hell, a place where the main agony was the knowledge that this refuge was allowed for a few hours a day only, and that the rest of hell might intrude itself at any time. In fact Jack's main activity was trying to prepare himself mentally for the terrors of the outside world.

From the bed, where he spent most of his time when he was not writing a paper for school, he could see his desk, which was covered with papers and half finished projects. Above his desk were some shelves upholding a chemistry set, a short wave radio receiver, some electronic parts, and some cheap plastic models, mostly of military vessels, which he had put together as a child and which his mother refused to let him remove. The walls of the room were beige.

Generally speaking, as long as he got A's in school and buried his nose in books at home his pain was minimized. Years of watching the family fight, the subdued hatred of his married forever parents for each other, the open fighting with his older brother, had made him almost catatonic with fear. There had been times when he imagined that his mother would flip out and murder them, and there were times when he considered whether he could get away with murdering them. Perhaps by turning on the gas stove at night and leaving a candle burning in the hall. He worried constantly that his mother would put poison in their food.

He would lie in his bed, reading. After getting home from school and eating he would often fall asleep, exhausted from four hours of swimming and a day of school. Then his mother would scold him, and demand that he study at his desk.

He lived with his brother and sister in a miniature police state. His mother opened his mail and read it before allowing him to see it. She frequently went through the drawers of the desks, seeking contraband. For that reason he was very careful what he wrote down. His one joy in life was that she had no idea what his thoughts were. His other joy was that, because she would not read them herself, she had no idea what was in the books he read, the ones by Asimov, Steinbeck, Heinlein, Faulkner, Thomas Wolfe, and the many science textbooks that he read.

His parents did not think anything was wrong with him, aside from sullenness. He knew otherwise. He was a psychological disaster area. It would be another year before he read an introductory psychology text and learned that there were words for him and his family: neurotic, psychotic, paranoid. He knew that the main emotion, really the only emotion in his life, was fear. He was afraid of his parents, the adults at school, his classmates, girls; he was afraid to drive a car, afraid to try drugs, afraid to rebel, afraid even to go to the neighborhood store and buy a gallon of milk. He suspected that his parents had created this mindset, but he was afraid that it might be a permanent part of him. The only things he was not afraid of were books and the jungle.

When he did not retreat into his books he retreated into the jungle. No one harassed him there if he did not count the mosquitoes, deer flies, and chiggers. Even in the heat he wore thick clothing to protect himself from the bugs. But they were part of the jungle, so it was ok, because the jungle was a whole. Without the mosquitoes more people would have been out there ruining things. He knew the trees, mostly oaks, holly, magnolia, hickory, palms, and cypress, with pine where it was drier. He knew the shrubs, the palmettos, the mushrooms and fungi that grew in the ground and on the fallen trees. There were anoles, small lizards that could change from green to brown at a moment's notice, and skinks with their lizard's racing stripes. You had to be fast and lucky to catch a skink. There were black snakes, corn snakes, green snakes, water snakes that you left alone because they looked like water moccasins, scarlet king snakes that looked like corral snakes and the rare corral snake itself with its nerve paralyzing venom, and rattlers. In the swamps there was an occasional alligator. In one pond there was a pair of otters. At night the raccoons and possums and armadillos came out. In the streams there were mud turtles. He knew the life in the ponds too, the dragon fly larvae with their enormous science fiction jaws, the tadpoles, newts, water boat men beatles. In the vernal pond behind the woods behind the community swimming pool, which filled up only when it was rainy, twice he was really lucky and caught some upside down swimming fairy shrimp. That was before they put in the golf course and then more roads and houses, destroying the wonderland of his youth.

 He would sit underneath some ancient tree beside the stream, wondering how people could be as screwed up as his parents. They were totally miserable. They were, by conventional standards, good people: hard working, did not drink or smoke, dad never beat mom, belonged to a major religious denomination. Totally miserable, totally sick, and wanting him to be that way too.

Frequently he walked to the flat lowland area beneath St. John's bluff, where it took little effort to find fossils. They were of recent times, geologically, when the area had been part of the atlantic ocean, now a good fifteen miles away. There were snail fossils and clams, sharks teeth, corals, and odd things that might have once been sponges or bryozoans.

He did not have a life of his own, but at least he was aware of it and did not like it. He planned on going away to college, and there he would begin to carve out a new life. There would be intelligent people to talk to, he would overcome his shyness and talk to girls and fall in love and quench his fevery sexual desire. Unless they locked him up for resisting the draft. They, the government, had wisely decreed that those who would be drafted to go off and kill people they did not know would register at the age of 18, when they were mostly still living with their parents. However, Jack had been skipped a grade in elementary school, so he would not have to register until he was away at college, and then his parents would not be able to make him. He was not half afraid of the FBI: he was used to prison. He did not believe he had anything over the gangs of black men chained together in blue prison suits who were forever clearing ditches along the roads as the school bus shuffled him from one prison to another.

In the morning he had to get up at six thirty to go to school. Most days as he stepped out the door he was overwhelmed by the stench from the paper mill that was across the river and miles away. Each year there were more roads, more shops, and more suburban houses laid out in what had only recently been empty sub-tropical jungle and swampland.

The Rolls School was a bad dream concretized in a bad reality. A chest high stone fence separated it from the boulevard artery which spewed forth the oxygen laden iron mobile cells into an asphalt capillary that, from the sky, outlined perfectly the symbol of the female sex, a circle with a cross below it. The boys, no girls attended it, who came in busses or in cars passed by a football field with bleachers on the left, then a baseball field on the right, a gym containing the old basketball court on the left, and then entered the circle counter clockwise past the classrooms, the dormitory for boarders, and then the new gym and pool complex as they completed the circle.

By his junior year Jack was accepted by the other denizens of this realized bad dream. No one bothered him as he sat in his seat on the bus studying or listening to the pop rock songs playing on the radio. No one picked on him any longer at school: playing water polo had made him one of the fellows. The rich kids, who were really mainly petite-bourgeois sons of doctors, lawyers, and merchants but passed for rich in Jack's book, had gotten used to his grey pants, white shirts, and clip-on ties. He had quickly caught up to and surpassed all but two or three of them in scholarship. Most of his friends were Jewish even though he was Catholic, but he got along OK with the protestants who were in the majority. It was 1971 and youth were united against The Establishment, which was still sending teenager boys off to die in South Vietnam.

Even the reactionaries were promising an end to the War. Nixon was touting his gradual withdrawal combined with Vietnamization; maybe he really believed that the South Vietnamese really hated the Viet Cong almost as much as they hated the White Devils from America. Of course in any large population you can find a range of opinion, and hear what you want to hear.

Jack and his friends were mostly thinking along the same lines at the Rolls School. They were overly protected by their parents and overly exposed to the world on TV. They had grown up with nuclear weapons and entered puberty with the Vietnam War in glorious technology color on evening TV. 35 Americans dead today, 935 Vietnamese. Heavy fighting near Hue. Their parents had plans for them: they would be businessmen, doctors, lawyers, Senators and Presidents. Many were considering becoming hippies, scholars, Hell's Angels, or most likely wondering if life was worth living. Five Hundred horny teenage boys all in one place, in a city and time and culture where girls were taught not to give in. They were supposed to be the next generation of leaders, like their Fathers before them. Fred's father was a State Assemblyman, Lawton Jr.'s a Senator, Tom's the local caddy dealer, Richard's a major construction contractor, Danny's the real estate developer who had sold a house to Jack's parents, McNeal's a doctor. They were supposed to support Mondale for President, no, it was another faceless con artist, Musky, or Scoop Jackson supposedly liberal on domestic issues and strong on Defense, or maybe even

Nixon, but most people, well white people, even rich white people, in Jacksonville would not admit to being a Republican, of the Party of Lincoln, the nigger lover, back then.

They began talking in the fall, before the first Vote in New Hampshire. Most of them were 18; their lottery numbers would come up the next year, to be drafted. Jack and his friends argued, Bruce for McGovern, Fred for Muskie, Jack for Birch Baye, Marty for Wallace, no one for Scoop Jackson. They talked about all the others, too: Shirley Chisolm, the black woman, a fire-eater by their standards; John Lindsay, Mayor of New York, a flaming liberal according to the local press; the possibility of Ted Kennedy running. No one said "maybe we should be like the Viet Cong," or the Black Panthers, or the Weatherpeople, but Jack was thinking that, probably Bruce and Lauren and some others were, too.

One person, Lauren, always wanted to talk about ecology, but no one else was interested back then.

There was only one thing they could all agree on: stopping the draft. Even the guys who did not want to stop the war weren't too keen on the draft. Oh, sure, some were brainwashed enough to think it was their duty to go if called, but no one was itching to be called. So by the time the school had a straw poll for the straw student democratic convention virtually all of the votes were either hard core conservative votes for George Wallace, who had a radical appeal in his own way, or liberal votes for George McGovern.

Jack was not very politically astute. He spent most of his childhood thinking politics was unimportant. His problem was religion, getting out from under the crushing weight of Catholicism; he had only the vaguest idea of what was happening in politics or in other nations. He did not read the newspaper and only watched the evening news when his father insisted on watching. At the Rolls School, however, his history professors inserted some current events into the curriculum. In ninth grade Mr. Blake had them play a game called Propaganda. He explained the different methods of propaganda: lying, omission, quoting authorities (who are lying or mistaken), flag waiving, taking quotes or facts out of context, etc. Jack, who was trying to figure out why his parents and the Catholic Church were so screwed up, and why people in the USSR were stupid enough to be Communists, learned this new game quickly.

His parents were New Deal democrats, getting more conservative as they aged. So the following year when Mr. Basetub took time from their Ancient History class to let the students argue about the race between Hubert Humphrey and Richard Nixon, Jack at first supported Humphrey, but he could not really say why. That was in 1968, the peak of the War in Vietnam, but Jack had not yet been personally affected by the war. He had heard that McCarthy, a supposed "peacenic" had challenged President Lyndon Johnson in the primaries and forced him out of the race, and had heard that there were riots at the Democratic Convention, but he knew little of the background or the details. Wars were meant to be won, America was a great democracy, and Nixon would win the war. He was not a wimp like Humphrey. The sons of the businessmen argued well for Nixon, and Jack decided he would have voted for Nixon if he could have voted.

But reality was hammering hard at the blinders and the ignorance. Every three weeks, when the last haul's books were due, one of his parents would drive him to the library downtown. Across the mighty St. Johns River, past streets lined with two story decrepit wooden houses with windows missing and swarming with black people, including lots of children running ragged and barefoot. Something was wrong with the great capitalist democracy: not every family had two cars, an air conditioner, and a garage. In fact there was the village of Cosmo only a half mile down the road from Jack's middle class neighborhood: every day on the way to school he would see the shacks and the half dead cars and the black skinned children dressed in clothes that were mostly the wrong size and faded, but clean. They were waiting for a bus that would take them to an all black public school.

Mr. Stop had attended Brown University and the students did not understand why he was teaching at the Rolls School. Mr. Stop was not sure either: he was not really a hippy or a radical, but he was not ready to become a junior manager at a bank, as Ivy League graduates are expected to. He had been a jock, even, and his football player's body and confidence made him an instant hit with most of his students. Jack read American History, faster than it was assigned, and began to be able to put his world, and the Vietnam War, in context. That year eight students showed up in black armbands on the day of the War Moratorium, and were sent home for it. Jack thought they were crazy, not because they opposed the war, but because they were willing to get in trouble to do it.

But he had started looking at the front page of the paper and paying more attention to the evening news. That summer, not having a way to get to a job, he spent studying, and more important, thinking. What was America doing in Vietnam? If we were fighting worldwide totalitarian communism, why didn't the Russians or Chinese fight alongside the North Vietnamese and Vietcong? And why were the Chinese Communists and the Soviet Communists at each other's throats? Why did he have to go to church when he was an atheist, and why had the blacks downtown rioted? Why were his parents living in a hell? Why couldn't he get information about sex? Why would his mother not let him play tackle football, or even touch, when she wanted him to go to the Naval Academy and become a Marine Corp officer and kill people for a living?

The liberals at Rolls could not agree on a candidate, but Fred's father was for Musky and he had a pretty good media image. The school administration announced that as an educational experience seniors who wished to would be allowed to go see Musky make a speech. They did not know it, but it was his first stop on a whistle stop train tour of Florida. Muskie had been surprised by McGovern and his kid brigades in Iowa and New Hampshire, so it was thought that if he didn't win the Florida primary he would be out of the running.

Even Fred was leaning to McGovern at that point, but an excuse to cut class is an excuse to cut class. Even the totally apolitical and Wallace supporters went. They were all in their nice preppy dress code, so they made a nice crowd for the television cameras.

Jack scoped out the reality: about 100 of his friends who were too young to vote, two men carrying unionist for Muskie type signs, and a bunch of reporters, listening to a boring speech by a man who was speaking to the cameras, not to them. The second most powerful, popular politician in the United States had no for real supporters in Jacksonville, Florida. Maybe he and Nixon had no for real supporters anywhere. Maybe the opposition could be like the Viet Cong.

Back at school, the students soon gravitated to supporting McGovern or Wallace.

Back at home the closest he ever got to his mother was watching her cook while waiting for dinner. He did not do this so much anymore; when he was younger it was his regular vulture's perch. Now he seldom caught even the last ten minutes or so, which was the waiting period. If the vegetables were frozen or from a can they would be dumped into pots to heat up; if fresh, they were already cooked beyond recognition. Some kind of meat would be sizzling in the electric frying pan or in the oven; the smell of it had brought him hungry to the kitchen. Mashed potatoes took only a minute, poured in flakes from a carton and whipped with margarine and milk. Only on holidays were they made from whole potatoes.

There were seven basic meals. Hamburgers with french fries. Fried chicken with mashed potatoes and gravy. Steak with baked potatoes. Barbecued chicken (baked chicken coated with bottled barbecue sauce) with biscuits or mashed potatoes. Pork with macaroni and cheese from a box. Taco casserole. Fish sticks with boiled potatoes. Any meal might be accompanied by any boiled vegetable.

Salvation was salads. His mother would take iceberg lettuce and break it up, cut up carrots, radishes, green peppers, and, when they could afford them, avocadoes, with raw green onions and make a dressing of oil and vinegar.

And daily he dreamed of sex love and of escaping off to college or even just to a job.

Chapter 4

ON THE ROAD

He had been camping twice before. Once was for a weekend during the two months that he belonged to the Boy Scouts of America. He remembered being taught how to build a fire, after he and his two friends had tried burning leaves and pinecones; being bored; and seeing that boyscouts was largely an excursion in telling racist and dirty jokes, smoking cigarettes, and being cruel to the weak.

The second time he had hitchhiked to a tiny state park and slept without shelter or fire, in order to avoid the ranger and paying the camping fee. He had left home by then.

This time he planned the trip carefully in advance. He was going into voluntary exile: he could take no more of the hypocrisy of civilization. He had been reading Carlos Casteneda's books (there were only two back then) and they were more interesting to him than work or school or rock and roll. He did not expect to find a shaman to guide him: he just wanted to look deep into himself and see if it were true that the mysteries of life were there. Meanwhile, since he was temporarily back at his parents' house, he borrowed his mother's sewing machine. After a bit of practice he began in on a kit he had bought to make the sack part of his backpack. Then he made a tiny tent of his own design, barely big enough for one person. By then he was quite good with the machine, and had no problem sewing a sleeping bag.

He took a train to Nashville (his parents insisted that he not hitch, and even paid for the ticket) and stayed a few days in a cheap hotel, visiting friends. Then he stepped out to the interstate, flagged down his first ride, and headed across the nation on Interstate 40.

The girl in the Volkswagen with her dog in the back seat let him off in Northern New Mexico, at Raton, where 87 met Interstate 25. She thought he was crazy to go off into the mountains with just a pair of $3 tennis shoes to walk in. He wondered about her, standing out on the interstate, as he began to get cold: the wind was blowing briskly. By his Florida calculations it was the beginning of March, and hence spring. He had figured on cold nights, but it was the middle of the day and even with his jacket on (only someone from Florida would have considered it a winter jacket) he was cold. He put on his gloves. His ears were freezing. A car went by: no dice. Colder. A half hour passed, another car went by. His ears were numb. He was getting worried.

The wind was tumbling a small dark mass towards him over the asphalt. He grabbed it as it came by. It was a blue knit hat! He made sure it had no bugs in it, then put it on. He could not see why such a thing would be blowing down the road. He considered himself charmed. More confident, he had also noticed that many more cars were taking a road that went off south of town than were coming along the interstate. He looked at his map: the road led to Taos. Lovey, his ex-girlfriend's roommate, had mentioned Taos as a wonderful place, a place of artists and hippies. He decided to try the road to Taos.

The walk to the road warmed him up. Almost immediately an old man, an Indian in an old blue ford, picked him up. He was just going to gather wood, so it was not a long ride. Standing alongside a narrow mountain road, cold again, he wondered as to how he could be so stupid. Fortunately, before he got frostbitten, a couple of german tourists picked him up. When they dropped him off to head to a ski area it began to snow and he began to freeze, but before long some Indians of about his own age picked him up, gave him a beer, and took him all the way into Taos.

By the evening of the next day he was where he wanted to be, in the Gila National Forest. He had bought some white flour, cornmeal, and oatmeal in a country store to supplement his other supplies. He had already done quite a bit of walking, carrying his backpack, and his legs were sore. He was exhausted, and he simply crawled into his sleeping bag and fell asleep.

He had bought topographic maps at the ranger station and proceeded on his hike the next morning. It was a continuous upward hike, around bend after bend. He knew from his map that the trail would reach a crest and then he could walk downhill to a stream. Every turn of the trail promised the crest. He had to rest more and more frequently. Well, at least it was warmer in the South of New Mexico than it had been in the North. And eventually he did come to the crest. When he came to the stream there were about 20 college students camped there: he moved just far enough along it to get out of earshot, made his camp, ate, and lay in his sleeping bag worrying about fiendish men and beasts.

When he had hiked for three days he stopped running into human beings altogether. Awaking at the dawn of the fifth day he found that he had camped near a cave. It was perfect: too open for beasts, but big enough for a man and a camp fire. Just in time, too: it began to snow again. So he could now have his freedom from human company, as long as he could stand it and forage up enough food.

The next day he walked downstream from the cave. He noticed there were trout in it, and began considering if being a vegetarian meant he should not each fish. It was not so much a matter of being an animal, as of eating another conscious being. He was not sure if he believed in Karma, or exactly what the rules of Karma were (was sex outside of marriage a sin for Hindus? He was not sure). The fish darted under rocks when he approached, but he found that his standing or sitting still allowed him to watch them come back out.

Returning to his camp in the afternoon he cut cattail shoots that were popping up along the stream and dug out dandelions. He cooked rice and lentils in his tiny pot, adding the greens at the end. He easily ate the entire pot. He contemplated that there was nothing to do, so he would be spending lots of time meditating. He had been taught Transcendental Meditation, which is simply the commercially packaged technique of repeating a word (un mot, mantra) in one's mind. He tried this, tried imagining various simple geometric images, he even tried concentrating on moving his compass with his mind.

As the weeks passed he grew hungrier and bored. He found he could catch the fish by simply turning over rocks to catch earthworms, putting them on a hook and line, and dangling them in front of the clearly visible fish. He thoughts turned to the possibilities back in society. He began to wonder if he had learned anything.

Five years later was 1979 and he was not really used to driving a car despite pretending to be an American male in his mid-twenties and a fan of Neal Cassidy if not Jack Kerouac. He had driven his red 1965 Valiant virtually not at all during his month in Seattle: city traffic confused him. Also, he was sure the car would break down at any moment: it drank a quart of oil every 50 miles and spewed great clouds of blue grey smoke out of the exhaust and the hood when it ran downhill. He had studied repair manuals, tightened bolts, and concluded the engine was lucky to move the car forward at all. He had been ripped off for 450 dollars, but there was nothing he could do about it. The car had gotten him from Washington D.C. to Seattle, and maybe it would get him to San Francisco.

It died as it labored up the hill on Interstate 5 in South Seattle. He pulled into the breakdown lane, opened the hood, could find nothing more wrong than usual. He closed the hood, got back in, turned the key, and the Valiant started and made it up the hill. He concluded it was his mind. After all, he had just been celibate for a month, not even beating off, suppressing his sexual thoughts as best he could.

When he got to Olympia he pulled off the highway and into the Dennys. He had put up a notice on the University of Washington ride board and had agreed to pick up a girl named Ricki and give her a ride to San Francisco. At first he did not see anyone with a backpack in the restaurant and almost left, but then he saw a girl with a backpack and asked her if she was Ricki. She had brown wavy hair, a small narrow plain face, and the voice he had found so attractive on the phone. He did not look at her much as they got loaded into the car.

"So what are you doing in Seattle?"

"Just travelling. I've got a couple more weeks."

She was easy to talk with. She had graduated from the University of Virginia and was touring the country, just as he was, in the late 1970's when the Age of Aquarius had turned sour but some people still had a restlessness. Her father was a nuclear engineer and had helped design the Three Mile Island nuclear power station that had melted down the year before. She liked the Grateful Dead and was radical and getting her head together. They talked continuously for eight hours before pulling into a state park to camp out for the evening. They slept in her tent, and he refrained from touching her.

The second night when he went back to the car to get a flashlight he smelled gasoline. There was a puddle of it under the car, and a small, steady stream spewing out of the bottom of the gas tank. He quickly got his tube of liquid aluminum, smeared some on a piece of cardboard, and held it up to the leak. He lay on his back, wondering how long he needed to hold it there and if it would do any good. Eventually she came over to ask what was happening. When he took his hand away the patch held in place. There was nothing else he could do right away.

The sky was clear so they did not bother to put up the tent. She suggested it would be more comfortable if they lay one sleeping bag out flat and then slept under the other, rather than each in their separate bags. He thought about the energy spilling out, a zen metaphor clear as day, but lay down with Ricki anyway. They talked awhile and then she said she did not mind being touched. They touched. They kissed. They made love.

That night he woke up and it was raining gently. He wondered if he should wake Ricki up and set up the tent, then he noticed he could see the stars. There was not a cloud in the sky, yet it was raining.

The redwood forests were so beautiful, it was like being with Eve or Lilith in paradise before love had become sin and hate a way of life. But they foolishly continued down the coast.

His emotions were mixed when Ricki got on the train in Berkeley to head back east a few days later; their time together hand been wonderful, but he could see how it could unravel if they tried to stay together. But he was worried, still not fully used to being alone in a new city and friendless, and his thoughts turned to finding a place to live. He was shocked to find out the price of even the sleazy hotels there, and decided to sleep in parks until he could find a place to rent. That night he parked his car in a ritzy section of Berkeley up the first hill. He took his sleeping bag and went off to find a place to sleep in the park in the hills. He did not know his way, and every time he tried to leave the road ended up running into thorns. He was exhausted by the time he found a dirt road leading into the park and then a reasonably level, clear patch of ground to lie down in.

In the light of the morning he could see Berkeley down below him, stretching to the bay. San Francisco lay in fog beyond that. He lay there a while, not wanting to expose himself to the cool of the morning. Reluctantly he emerged from the sleeping bag, slipped into his clothes, and stuffed his bag into its sack. The poncho that he had used as a ground cloth was sticky with dew, dirt, and leaves. He walked down the hill and back to his car, where he stashed his bags and ate a breakfast of bread and peanut butter.

He walked down Telegraph Avenue, taking in the people, himself an inconspicuous arrival with short hair, jean pants and jacket. When he reached the Berkeley campus he turned left, down the hill. At the bottom of the hill he noticed a sign about meditation in the window of a building. Soon he had reached Shattuck Avenue and found out that the library was not yet open. He found a small park and waited. When the library opened he went to the magazine shelves and began catching up on his favorites.

Days passed, an alternation of walking and exploring, sitting in the library reading or writing, and sleeping in the car or the hills. After three days there was a notice on the windshield of his car saying his car was presumed abandoned and would be towed if he did not move it. He was angry and considered breaking the windows of the house which he had parked in front of; the owner had doubtless called the police. So he moved the car a bit every few days. He wondered what would have happened if it had needed a repair to start it up.

There were not many rooms for rent that met his bohemian budget. He checked every bulletin board he could find and figured he was either going to use up his money quickly, would have to get a job, or would move on to Mexico. Then he saw a note in the laundromat on College Avenue, hand written, about a real cheap room. $85 a month in a group house.

The first time he saw Marie, when he went to interview to rent the room, he thought she was fifty years old. She was in the kitchen with Cayenne, Julie, Babs and Ken. Babs and Ken were filthy and sweaty from work; they and Cayenne looked about 30 years old, just beginning to show wrinkles. Julie had put up the ad and was moving out: she was twenty years old. The conversation did not seem to be going anywhere; he gathered they were all artists who had to work for a living. They talked more about the pain of work than art. He said he was writing; he avoided saying what. The room would not be available for a while anyway. The only thing that was weird, considering that it was a house of artists, was that Cayenne and Marie spent some time smooching.

The next time he saw Marie she looked closer to forty, and he thought he must have been projecting or misinterpreting the first time. Both times she had trouble speaking, as if she were mentally deficient. The second time, though, she seemed more together and talked to him at length, explaining that she had had a small cancer removed from her hand and could not use it well yet. Since he had spent the intervening three weeks in the street and had only bathed once in that time, he was not feeling very superior to her. She was living on social security payments for mental disability.

The next thing he knew his girlfriend, who was spending a year at school in Chicago, called to say she was dating someone else. He knew the scoop: back to Chicago, get a job, go straight, or she would drop him. He loved her, but knew she was too straight for him. It was going to bend them both out of shape, it was going to end sometime. But when she called and said she had slept with her new beau and it was over he cried. He still had his consciousness to work on, he had his zen, he had a black depression.

His mind was in such bad shape he could not deal with getting his car running. If it were running o.k. it would be worth a few hundred dollars, or he could drive it somewhere. He concluded that it needed a new cylinder head gasket, at the very least, and probably it needed to have the cylinders rebored or new rings. Certainly if it had not needed reboring when he got it his driving it without oil in Chicago for a few miles had caused the necessary damage. Doing such a job himself would require tools he did not own and did not know how to use.

Fear was something he had hoped to leave behind, but now it reasserted itself in a strange way. He opened up the engine to see if he could judge the extent of the damage and whether it was worth fixing. In the course of this he discovered that the main source of oil leakage was a missing bolt that should have been helping to hold on the generator. The cylinders were in bad shape, but at least the car would not need so much oil. All he had to do was put in a new gasket put the upper block back on. But he did not know what size engine he had, in fact the only things he was sure of were that it had six cylinders and was not a Valiant engine. He had never tried to buy a part at a real auto parts store before, just at department stores. He would have to either get a gasket and try it and pay for others if the first did not fit, or get the parts person to look at the engine and maybe guess right. The idea of doing either struck a deep note of fear. He knew this was irrational, but it was always easy to put off doing it until another day: he had nothing but time. Finally, he checked the car again and the insides had rusted frozen; the car had truly become junk. So much for the Cassidy routine.

In the meantime a number of characters had come and gone at Grace Street, but only Baggins, that is right, Bilbo Baggins, had managed to attach himself. Like a tick burrowed into the back of the neck. It was not Jack's fault; unlike the other house members he was far from open handed. Baggins had been brought home as a boyfriend of Sonya, who was devastatingly beautiful and Marie's daughter. Sonya was living in the street, or with whatever boyfriend or drug dealer or party thrower took her in for the night. Often she stayed at Grace Street, but she did not abuse the privilege. She was not mean, she just had no direction in life, at least not in the ordinary sense. She took drugs, did tarot readings, and wrote poetry. And she brought Baggins home.

Baggins had a beard of curly dark brown hair, the face of a forty year old man, some broken teeth, and an incomprehensible mumbling voice. His brain was fried to a crisp from using drugs; psychedelics were his favorites. He was a competent tailor and had a scheme for supporting himself: making denim long-tailed tuxes and tophats. He was wearing one most of the time, it was quite charming, pure satire and perfect if belated hippy. They would use the toolshed behind the house and borrow Marie's sewing machine. They would get the denim out of Berkeley's free boxes. He was selling the suits for $45 a piece and already had an order. It would be pure profit.

Jack and his housemates gave him dinner and agreed he could use the toolshed. Cayenne made sure it was clear that they would not use the toolshed to crash in, only to work in. Cayenne did not ask for rent, but Baggins agreed to pay some anyway, as soon as he sold some suits.

It was not long before he and Sonya were living in the shed, and Baggins stayed there even when Sonya got a new boyfriend. He would sneak into the kitchen when no one was there, or if Marie was there, since she could not refuse anyone food. He was always about to pay rent, always about to sell a suit or make some profit in a drug deal. But when he did buy a suit he attempted to enlarge his fortune by buying some drugs to resell, but he was already at the retail level and ended up taking the drugs himself and the house were lucky to get some of the drugs out of him. Jack was totally off drugs, so he considered Baggins one big pain.

One way they kept their food bills down, kept the ticks from sucking them dry, was the sauce. They had moved some furniture for the lady next store and in return she gave them a gallon can of jalapenos. Cayenne took the peppers and half filled a blender with them, then added raw onions, garlic and tomatoes. The knives whirled and the sauce was born: it filled a gallon jug and a few quart jars.

At first it was used with some moderation, added to tacos, sandwiches, that sort of thing. Then it began to be incorporated into omelets and stews and casseroles. Jack ended up spreading it on toast. Gradually it became a flavor missed if not strongly present. They even put it in spaghetti.

It was Cayenne who taught Jack how to make proper spaghetti. The secret was to fill a pot with water and put it on the flame first. While it was getting to boiling Cayenne would start hamburger frying, then chop onions, celery and garlic, adding them to the pan as they were chopped. When the water boiled the spaghetti noodles went in, leaving ten minutes to get the sauce cooked and add the tomato paste and, of course, the jalapenos sauce.

Everybody knew the amount of methedrine that a freak took just to get half sober would kill an ordinary person. That's how it was with the sauce. They could hardly taste it in the spaghetti sauce, but people who came over for a free meal would quickly find their throats on fire. If they continued eating their entire body was soon aflame. If that did not convince them to eat elsewhere the sauce leaving their bowels the next day would.

One day in the spring Jack was getting ready to walk to Berkeley and Baggins latched on to him. The last thing Jack wanted was to walk into Berkeley along with someone dressed in a denim tux with top hat, carrying a very large, almost man sized duffle bag filled with clothing that would certainly have to be shared, whose voice was seldom coherent enough to make sense out of. But there was no escaping it: if he was walking to Berkeley, Baggins was walking with him.

Baggins was holding his thumb out as he walked but paying no attention to traffic. There was a honk and Jack spotted a van with a woman leaning out of the passenger window offering a ride. He told Bilbo, who did not respond, and then grabbed him, pointed, and pulled. They ran across two lanes of traffic to where the van had stopped and was waiting for a light.

Time warp. Tie dyed window curtains, leopard skin rug, Grateful Dead music, beads, a Buddha, pictures of Indian deities. The occupants asked directions to a place in Oakland, two young beautiful glowing faced long haired women and a young, perhaps college aged man. They were going away from their destination, so they continued on their path to drop off Bilbo and Jack in Berkeley. Jack, entranced by the women, celibate for six months, offered to stay with them until they found their destination; he figured they were stoned and would otherwise wander around the bardo of Oakland Berkeley for an eternity. They were going to some sort of store.

They asked him if he liked the Grateful Dead and he said they were one of his favorite bands. He got their names, Vicki and Tamar and Tim, and learned that they were Deadheads. Serious. The van, a Chevy, belonged to Vicki. When she gave him The Look, which he had not experienced before, he thought he would melt.

When they had obtained whatever obscure article they were looking for they asked him if he wanted to go to a Grateful Dead concert. He said he was low on money, but sure, why not. They assured him that they were very close to the Dead and could probably get him in free. He said o.k. When was the concert? In three days, they said. Did he want to get high?

Stoned, he considered his luck. He did not want to get his hopes up too high, but these looked like very fine women. The Dead really were his favorite band, and he had always wondered what they were really like. Perhaps he would get to meet them.

"How quickly can you get ready?" asked Vicki.

"Get ready for what?"

"We want to leave for the concert this afternoon."

"Why? Where is it?"

"The first one is in Illinois somewhere." "Well, I guess it would only take a few minutes to pack, and I'd need to go to the bank and get some money."

"How much money do you have?"

"How much do you think I'll need?"

"Well, if you had twenty or thirty dollars to pay for gas that would be great."

"I'll get thirty. I can manage that."

"Great. Give us your address and we'll pick you up around three."

A few hours later he was in the van with nine people heading to Illinois. If they drove continuously they would get there for the beginning of the concert. A tape of a previous Dead Concert was playing. Everyone except Jack knew it was the tape of the 1977 New Years Concert in Oakland; they knew because such knowledge was coin of the realm in the land of the Dead.

They had enough Acid, (LSD, lysergic acid Diethylamide, a harmless though potent hallucinogen derived from the ergot fungus) in the van to send them collectively to jail for the rest of their lives. Someone had a cold and wanted to get some tissues before getting on the freeway, and did not want to pay for them, so they stopped at a McDonald's, but accidentally drove into the drive-in take out lane, with three cars ahead of them and, immediately two cars behind them. It took ten minutes to get through the line, but then they managed to get on the freeway. The tape churned into a slow rendition of "Sugar Magnolia". A hemp cigarette made the rounds. Jack had been abstaining from drugs, but figured he had better share it if he wanted to survive the trip.

They travelled across California in the dark of night, tape after tape threading its electromagnetic way through the player and into acoustic space and well worn ears. Jack liked the music, he felt music deprived, but it was not clear enough in the van to really enjoy. He took a turn driving, headlights piercing air and asphalt, on and on. He paid for gasoline. He learned that a picture of a guru, Yuktananda or something like that, was supposed to keep the engine from breaking down. Anything is possible in the Twilight Zone. He did not sleep. He lusted after the three women in the Van.

They entered Nevada in the morning before the dawn. As those who managed to sleep began to awaken the reality of having so many people in a tiny space began to work its alchemy on various consciousnesses. The Dharma Nuns who needed the others to help pay for gas began to suspect that their nerves would fray later on. The middle class heads could not help that their substrates were unhappy at not being treated like princes. Talk turned immediately to various past Grateful Dead concerts. Jack watched the scenery. The sun beat down on the desert, and on the van. A joint was lit, passed around, and returned to dust.

Lunch was a horror. Dried seaweed, sunflower seeds, sesame tahini, vegetables and fruit. Afternoon was heat, but they started climbing out of the desert into the mountains. Digger explained that the Diggers were hippy communists who helped organize the San Francisco communal houses during the 60's. They in turn had taken their name from the Diggers of late medieval England, who had rejected Catholicism and practiced communal farming and the seizure of land from the feudal lords. This all sounded great to the middle class heads, who were rejecting materialism, since wealth had brought them and their parent only unhappiness.

By the time they reached Illinois not only were various heads disenchanted with one another, but no one was copping to holding any money; it had all been spent on gas and food. To get into the concert itself they would either have to crash the gate or sell LSD. Jack decided he might as well see the concert, so he found a buyer for the 1/8 gram of crystal methedrine he had brought along for just such emergencies. The concert was outdoors, in a fenced in area, with security guards, mostly people younger than Jack, stationed every few yards along the fence.

The Grateful Dead played their spacey intricate country– western–blues–jazz music and pretty soon it began to rain. People played in the mud, the band played on. Jack guessed that the LSD most of his friends were carrying would be ruined by the rain. He was right: several hundred dollars worth of acid went down the drain because no one had bothered to wrap it in plastic. He had had enough of the fools. The next day he started hitching back to Berkeley; the Dead Heads somehow got a tank of gas together and headed towards Chicago.

Chapter 5

WAGE SLAVERY

Paranoid. Something is going to go wrong. Terror. Your heart will stop. You are secretly infested with syphilis and are about to go insane. You will suddenly be unable to breath. Your mother will call. The cops will walk in. Your girlfriend will be affected by the drug, go berserk, and stab you to death with a butter knife. There is paraquat in the leaf and you are about to have your nervous system fried. Something you ate for lunch, it must have been the three day old, sour smelling brown rice, and you are about to be sick. You will strangle on your own vomit. At heart you are rotten and due a hellish end.

It passes, lifting away like a fog, only to linger as a ceiling of clouds or a wisp in the sky or horror over the horizon. There's nothing metaphysical about it, it's a real world. The fact that you are actually going to continue to breath is almost irrelevant. Nothing is even really different, the world and its colors and shapes are the same, but obviously your mind is being affected, your emotions are thrashing around, your memory is tied in knots, and the most amazing thought just occurred to you.

It's not like when you were child and you lay flying on your bed over the dreamlands. It's an involved thought that sucks in you consciousness the same way a good movie or book or dream does: as if you could touch understanding with mental hands. Flying with the world, harmonious, hilarious.

And then you can't remember it. That is the catch. Gone. So you put on the stereo and halfway fall asleep and in the refrain of "Rain" the needle skips forward all the way to the final cut. You consider the possibilities: a scratch, a truck going by outside, and earthquake, your mind. The next day you look in the paper but no earthquake was reported.

Fear and loathing in America. 1968: driving by the black tenements when Dad or Mom drove you to the library. 1972: little black kids at the public swimming pool hugging the lifeguards' legs and covered with ill healed scars. 1974: job at a factory paying $2.25 an hour, and in the paycheck most of that disappears much like the corn crop of a medieval surf. Rent is a more pressing reality than fine points of Wittgenstein. Old women doing piecework, their hands moving faster than Houdini's because a missed beat means a missing finger.

The moment of creation is the closest thing to magic that exists in the real world. Some drugs place you there for the briefest time, and you think the drugs are a reliable way to get there. You take more drugs. They have side effects. You are sliding down a chute towards a machine that chops up fish.

But it passes. There's always a dollar when you need it, if you are willing to stoop low enough. It would be easier to rationalize if your mind were not in tow.

The moment of creation is the closest thing to magic that exists in the real world. That is why rich people flock around artists like deerfly in summer. The Vampire Lestat was merely reversing the roles when he related the story of the Vampires putting on shows for the delight of Parisian society. The vampires sat there, in their finery, hoping for a moment of creation, a moment of genuine consciousness, to be radiated out and sucked up. $60 for a broadway show is a bargain, especially if you didn't have to earn it to begin with.

Fortunately the main result is that pseudo artists swarm about rich people like vultures around carrion. Mostly the pseudo artists are the financially semi-disenfranchised children of the rich and the near rich, and capable of a modicum of creativity by the circumstances of their upbringing and finances. They want the recognition their parents denied them, and for this they exert themselves.

It was not a long walk. Down to Wickenden Street, across the bridge, a left turn, a right turn. The factory was a gigantic four story shed with ancient lattice windows that had never been cleaned topped by exhaust fans that had to work if people were to walk out alive. It was summer but not hot early in the morning: he wore a long sleeve shirt that he hoped would protect him from tiny fragments of reality flying at skin piercing speed. He was apprehensive: it was his first job other than working at a swimming pool. He had asked for a job at every place in town he could think to ask at. He expected a line of men with lunch pails at the factory gate, but none were in sight. He went into the office and announced himself.

Have a seat. Wait. Fake hardwood panelling. Cheap barely padded metal chairs. Time. Serving time. There are others, two others, but no one talks. Even at Auschwitz people talked, but not here. No one has pointed a gun at their heads: it is not something to chat about here. Maybe inside.

The door opens but one of the other men is asked in first. The door opens again and a greying dark haired man in a tie asks you to come in. He asks you how you are, says he's glad to have you aboard and hands you to a grey haired keeper of the forms. They just need a W-4. Another wait and a fat man right out of the beer drinking commercials comes and leads you through dark metal halls of noise to a high ceilinged dingy chamber of clanking machines. Overhead a collection of pipes waits ready to sprinkle a fire, allows constant movement of production fluids, and intermingles with electrical cables, lighting fixtures, and odd structural steels.

Many of the machines are unattended, but at some a human being stands or sits, and a small man who is the floor manager, not wearing a tie, comes up, says his name which you cannot hear, and takes you over to a machine. There he introduces Joe the grey haired fatherly foreman. Joe walks away and the manager sits down in the machine's seat and explains in a loud voice that cannot be heard over the machines that you are making lengths of copper ribbon. He points to the marker that you pull the ribbon, which is an inch wide, up to. He points to a pedal, kicks it with his foot, and the upper structure of the machine comes crashing down and cuts the ribbon. He puts it in the box to the left with a bunch of other pieces and does the operation again a few times. He asks if you understand. He gets up and you sit down, thinking that it is easy enough except that there is no guard to keep your fingers from being chopped off, and you pull the ribbon through the guide to the marker, pull back your hands, and kick the pedal.

The strip of copper is fine and you put it in the box along with the other strips. You pull at the copper again, get it in place, kick the pedal. The machine crashes again and you put the strip of copper in the box along with the other strips. You do it again, then again. Finally the manager says that you are doing fine and he walks away.

Strip after strip accumulates in the box. It is boring, you wonder how you are going to make it through the day. Eternity passes, you have counted to one hundred a few times. You look up and stretch your neck around to see the clock. Ten minutes have passed since you sat down.

You look around as much as you can without losing a finger or two. Everyone else has already checked you out: their movements are as automatic as the machine's, they can look even as their hands fly to make jewelry. They pegged you the moment you walked in: Anglo kid, bound to quit soon.

Somehow the day comes to an end and you walk back to your apartment you are sharing with two students and one photographer and try to make sense of your life. Having grown up with just one cut above the industrial proletariat, having some hope in them from two years of political science and a touch of Marx and Lenin, there is little to say.

The days begin with a walk through Fox Point into South Providence. The other students can live off their parents or get jobs of a more dignified and lucrative nature, but Jack is an outcast, he has refused to buckle, and now he must pay the price. He lines up with the others at the gate, long haired but broken. He looks at his watch: he hates being even a minute early, but to be a minute late means getting docked for a quarter hour. He rushes in and pulls out his card, stabs it in the time machine, and goes to the roll of copper ribbon.

At lunch breaks all the women in the machine room talk to each other in rapid Italian and the few men talk about sports and what was on TV last night. Jack reads while he munches on a sandwich. One day he brings a copy of a work by Lenin in, it seems appropriate in a factory, and the other young worker, whom he hasn't spoken at all to, sees it during lunch and announces that he is a member of the Attica Free Brigade and they have guns. Jack avoids him after that: it doesn't show good sense to say something like that to someone you don't know.

The copper strips, ten thousand of them, get taken to another machine for Jack to make right angle bends in them. Then He makes the same number of copper plates. Then he punches holes in them. Then he learns they are going to be ornamental belt buckles for the marine corp. The factory closes for one week each summer, for him it is unpaid vacation, and he called in sick the next monday and never went back. It was time to march down to the interstate, stick out his thumb, and see Amerika.

Amerika (in 1974) is Lila's between downtown Nashville and Vanderbuilt University. The sign says Rooms for Rent, day, weekly, monthly. You know you have to get an apartment, but you don't have enough money to stay in a hotel in the meantime. Lila is long gone but a skinny heavily made up woman says the cheapest room is nine dollars a night or twenty-four dollars a week or eighty dollars a month. You pay for a week. The room has a bed, a kitchenette, and a shower: the toilet is in the hall. What the hell.

It is a recession, the Nixon recession, and jobs are hard to come by. Everything pays minimum wage and there are six hundred applicants for every position. Someone says try Caesar's Pizza, next to the university, and they hire you to fill in three nights a week. One night you are a sandwich cook, minimum wage, and two other nights you wait on tables, no wage, just tips. The manager thinks you look honest, will get along with the students, and, anyway, no one else wants the job. No six hundred applicants here, just three or four every day.

Back at Lila's the old people listen to radio preachers and the ladies offer their services for a fee you can't afford and they can't live on. No one, including you, cleans up the bathroom. Roaches, hundreds of them, swarm over the room even before you turn off the lights at night.

The other workers at the Italian Restaurant are cool. They smoke dope and hang out together sometimes, they can't go to fancy clubs on their wages. The customers often don't leave tips because even though they are waited on they are using plastic forks to eat their manicotti.

Also, on more than one occasion the manicotti or lasagna is still frozen at the center when the guests cut into it. The problem is that on busy nights it pays to not leave the factory prepared, frozen entrees in the microwave more than the regulation time. Usually they come out fine, but on occasion the radiation doesn't do the job. The outsides are hot, but the centers are ice. Slop on some of Caesar's homemade sauce and go for that sandwich order: slice the bread, stuff in the meat, pop it in the microwave, and again, and again.

The restaurant owner is rich and getting richer. The pay at Caesar's, about $60 a week take home until you can get more shifts, won't go far so you decide to look for a full time job during the day.

Jobs are hard to find, but this one ad wants someone who can read blueprints. What could be hard about that? Joe hires you because you are from back east and so is he. Maybe he recognizes your Catholic School mannerisms. For some reason some people like you. So you come into this big warehouse and in the back is the area where the machines are put together. The first thing you work on is this slitting and perforating machine which is for making things like checks – it makes the little holes that, supposedly, allow the check to tear out of the booklet. It is very simple in conception – it picks up a piece of paper, runs it under a wheel that makes the punctures with its teeth, and stacks the perforated paper on the other side. It has a fair number of parts that make up its supporting structure, power chain, and paper movers. The first thing Jack has to do is tighten a nut, and he doesn't even know whether tightening is clockwise or counterclockwise, and he is all thumbs and takes about five times as long to do it as he would even a few days later. Joe looks dubious.

After a couple of days of bolting pieces together they have a working machine. Gradually Jack graduates to making sub-assemblies without Joe's supervision, and then to making whole machines from blueprints. In the process he learns to ream out bolt holes, create threads for machine screws, and get poorly machined parts to fit together. He also learns the Joe is a true believer. When Joe came home from the war and could not find a job, he got to despairing, but then he had a vision of the Virgin Mary, who told him he would soon meet his wife, and soon thereafter met his wife and got married.

In five weeks it is obvious that Jack is not going to learn anything more. He has already quit at the restaurant. Joe invited him to come over for Christmas dinner. That was enough to send Jack flying.

What the hell, why not go back to college. If you have to work why not get paid for it? Only the main activity of that year of college is taking LSD, and by graduation you don't want to work at all: breathing, walking, thinking are all chores. Pretending to want jobs at interviews does not wash, and the Vietnam war is over and the Carter Recession is now in full flower: no jobs for anyone, much less walking zen koans.

Tom lives next door and has become a friend. A Brown dropout, he loves books, munchies, marijuana, basketball, and Saturday Night Live. He lives on unemployment, but it is going to run out. He and some friends heard there are jobs in Wyoming: lots of jobs, a real shortage of bodies, good wages. They buy a tent, fix up the Valiant a bit and head west. But Jack stays behind, hoping for a job from the feds, in the meantime getting $120 a month unemployment, of which $55 goes to rent his room in the group house, and $45 a month for food; he would spend less, living on rice and beans, but his housemates have more money and they do the food communally. Jack does not care, at least he does not have to work for a while. If he isn't hanging out, talking to Patty or Steve or Molly or Lloyd or Tom or any of a number of people, smoking dope perhaps and listening to vinyl, he is wandering the streets of Providence, lost in imagination.

Yes, there is work in Wyoming, $5.00 an hour with plenty of overtime. What the hell. A bus ticket is $55, pack the backpack and sleeping bag, cook some marijuana brownies (having been on a cross country bus journey before) and take a book and notebook to stave off discomfort and boredom. America from a bus for 3 days: forest, farms, and franchises. People who are too poor to take planes, some of them plain honest folk, some walking mental or physical disaster areas.

After a couple of misdirections Jack manages to walk from the bus station in Gillette, Wyoming to Camp Cody, which is close enough to the interstate to hear its scant traffic and far enough from town that the walk is an inconvenience. Inside its fences, behind the buildings housing the manager, her office, and the communal bathrooms, are a number of cars parked next to tents, pickup campers, and RVs. He recognizes his friends' tent, but they are not there, all he can do is wait. His friends arrive back, half dead, from work around 7 p.m., even though it is Sunday.

5 a.m. the next morning the alarm goes off. Jack, fresh, has less trouble than the others getting up; Tom is the worst, they practically have to force him up and into the car. They leave at 5:20 for the drive out into the desert. The land is rolling rather than flat, a pockmarked with sage and other desert plants. There is almost no traffic on the back roads. They park near a railroad track with some other cars. Men, no women, are lounging around. Tom introduces Jack to the foreman, Shorty. Shorty gets out a W-4 tax form and Jack signs it. Then Jack is given a hard hat and is added to a team where one of the people has not shown up.

There are already ties and rails down and spikes in place. Jack is given a 70 lb nipping bar, essentially a crowbar about the height of a man and over an inch in diameter, and is shown how to wedge it under a wooden tie and then press down on it. A mobile pneumatic hammer that rides the rail then smashes down the spike into the wood, securing the rail, but only if Jack is able to push downward on the nipping bar with sufficient pressure to force the wood up against the blows of the hammer. One spike done, his body jarred by the vibrations, Jack pulls the bar out and inserts it under the next tie. Again the blows of the hammer are transmitted from spike to wood to nipping bar to Jack's flesh.

It takes a major effort to move the nipping bar, it is so heavy. In ten minutes Jack's muscles ache so badly he wonders how long it is possible to do this. His teammates do not tell him that the job is normally rotated; they have dumped the worst position on him. Soon his body is numb. Then, an eternity later, they have reached the end of the rail, and he has a moment's respite.

It is the mid-1970's but almost everything is done by hand. The workers use tongs to set the heavy wooden ties in place. Then the plates, dumped out on the ground from a truck, are carried and laid on the ties where the rail will fall. The rail itself, a quarter mile long, is pulled from a flatbed railcar by the concerted effort of the entire gang of workers onto rollers which suspend it over the ties until they are knocked over.

Even the easiest job, placing the spikes and giving them a few taps with a hammer to set them in the wood, is backbreaking. At the end of the first day

Jack's entire body is numb and in pain. Back at camp he cannot do his yoga stretches, his muscles are so cramped.

$5.00 an hour, twelve hours a day, seven days a week. After four or five days Jack's body is no longer in continuous pain, but the work is never easy. There's no chance to talk to the other guys; the work is too hard. For lunch Jack, Tom, Jake and Tim run to their car to try to wolf down enough food to keep them going for the afternoon. What few words that do get exchanged are not encouraging. Leadville, the old guy with the wired shut jaw, was walking along when a jack holding up a rail shot loose, smashing his jaw. They took him to the hospital, wired him up, and he was back at work the next day. Getting workman's compensation or even unemployment is nearly impossible in Wyoming. Plenty of work for everyone (back then, before too many people moved there, looking for work, and they finished building the new coal mines). Work you till you die.

If you've been a field nigger and luck promotes you to house nigger at first it seems like you've been set free. Then, usually pretty quickly, you realize you are a well paid slave. But at least, like Nat Turner, you get to see the inside of the master's house and get to know the masters' weaknesses.

To his surprise Jack was promoted to house nigger and did not even have to cut his hair. It was in Washington, D.C.; as part of collecting unemployment he had to apply to three jobs a week. One place gave him an interview and, when two people quit on them four months later, hired him.

His job was to call up doctor's offices when they failed to report as required on the Intraocular Lens

Product. Joyce, a tall, black woman of about his age who he immediately developed a crush for (but always carefully hid, especially after learning she was a Christian) showed him how the forms were supposed to be filled out, then gave him a four inch thick data printout that mostly indicated where doctors had "started the patient's clinical trial" and then failed to file follow up reports.

Nine or so people besides Jack worked on the exact same job, and the total employees for the project totalled about 20. His employer owed his new found wealth to the Dalcon Shield. That was an IUD that a greedy doctor and pharmaceutical company had pawned off on women who didn't want their emotions fucked with by The Pill but wanted a more reliable form of birth control than the diaphragm. The shield was not tested before being mass manufactured and distributed; it turned out to be a breeding ground for bacteria, and killed and seriously injured hundreds of women before being withdrawn from the market. Now there was legislation requiring that not only drugs but medical devices be tested and then approved by the FDA before they were allowed to go to market.

The FDA decided that intraocular lenses, which are like contact lenses implanted inside the eye to replace the natural lens when it is damaged, would be subject to testing. This despite the fact that they had been safely used for years. Only about 100,000 people a year were already having the lenses implanted, and people did not want to sit around blind for five or ten years while the FDA did its thing. So Jack among hundreds of others, was wasting his time pretending that they were doing a useful scientific with a sample size of 100,000 trials per year: the FDA had declared that every single person receiving an intraocular lens would be treated as an experimental subject.

But the people at work were good and fun people. It was the first place he had worked where black skinned people were hired on an equal basis; just about everyone there was cool, even the bosses. Still, the job itself was boring and pointless, except that he had graduated to domestic slave status.

Twelve years later the winds of chance blew Jack into the office of Beastridge Temp's off Interstate 8 in San Diablo. He'd seen everything: factories and offices, men and women of all shapes, sizes, colors and dispositions, the resignation of a President about to be impeached, riots, the insides of jails, the insides of drug deliriums, the salons of the rich and poor and middle class. He could write computer programs in 6 languages, was better at law than many lawyers, and was on Cointelpro's list as a dangerous writer and political organizer. But it is the sixth year of the Reagan Recession, billed by the lying with statistics crowd as the fifth year of the Reagan Recovery, and all they wanted to know was how fast could he type.

They advertised for paralegals and legal secretaries, but it was a lie: they wanted bodies. Jack had never typed over 50 words per minute in his life, but the well dressed proto-yuppie girl who interviewed him glanced at his test and said he did 65.

The following Monday, a tall white woman with dark hair, greeted him at the American Bloody Cross in Hillcrest. He had agreed to work for $8 an hour, which might cover expenses until he could find a better job. The woman took him upstairs to the Marketing and Communications department. Mary, the department head, is not in, but he was introduced to Peter and Tom, both of whom seem nice, and Mary, a dark pretty woman who spokes with an accent. Then he waited until Sandra came in. She seemed nice and gives him something to do.

It was a good job except for the pay. It was easy compared to what he had had to do in the past: just a bit of typing, organizing and answering the phone. Everyone in the department is really nice. The equipment is obsolete, so it takes a long time to get work done, but that is fine. The work gets done. It is mostly fundraising letters and news releases.

Anyway, it was only supposed to last for a couple of weeks, then off to the next assignment. It beat working for lawyers or corpos. People called and Jack begins fielding the simpler information calls. Does the Bloody Cross help the homeless? Only if they lost their housing due to a fire or other disaster. What else does it do? It teaches first aid, it has a program called Wheels that moves old and incapacitated people around, it responds to disasters, it provides services to the military and dependents. Where does its money come from? Mainly the United Fund and people who want to help victims of disasters. Wheels and the WIC program are funded by federal grants, the fees for the first aid courses pay for them.

Disasters are rare, and a couple of million dollars a year in United Funds payments extorted from workers subsidizes the military in San Diablo, a hidden prop to the government's defense budget. The rest of the money goes to pay $80,000 a year to the head parasite and $50,000 a year to the second in command, while the volunteers get nothing and the clerical staff gets dismal wages. Most of the regular employees were paid less than Jack was.

Anyone unhappy? The average turnover was one person a week from paid staff; even law firms that size don't have such bad turnovers. As the weeks passed Jack felt increasingly ripped off: he had signed up for legal jobs that were supposed to pay $9–12 an hour and he was getting $8, and he found out that Beastridge was getting $12.80. That meant every week Beastridge earned 40 x $4.80 = $192 a week off his back without lifting a finger.

Finally Mary left: she had had enough. Jack asked the Bloody Cross to hire him as a freelancer, and they not only refused, but, when he left, told Beastridge. Beastridge then told the Association of Temporary Agencies and Jack was blacklisted. And he had not even started a union. Yet.

Chapter 6

ROCK AND ROLL

There was no helping waking up when Snark came in at five in the morning. He tried to be quiet but the sheet of fiberboard that partitioned Jack's room did not block sounds at all. Also, it was still in the night lull: before Jack fell back asleep he heard the M train roll underneath the building. Cars and trucks passed on Delancey and Allen streets noisy but singly or in small clumps: there were moments of near silence.

The alarm went off and he hit it quickly. Cracks between the fiberboard and the floor and the ceiling admitted ample light to see by. His single bed took up most of the room; his clothes hung from a horizontal pole at the end away from the door, a homemade desk and an assemble-yourself steel bookshelf took up the rest of the room. He opened the door on the "living room" and waded around stacks of corrugated cardboard boxes filled with records that either Iman had not unpacked or had packed and not yet shipped. The room was bright with sunlight: the loft's south wall was all windows. He showered to wake up and shaved in the shower.

The kitchen was next to the bathroom. It had a half-dead refrigerator, a stove, sink and counter. He beat an egg in a bowl, added flour, powdered milk, caraway seeds, and baking soda. He heated a skillet as he beat water into the mixture. He dumped it in the pan. Half-asleep, he watched it expand slowly. He flipped it over, pleased that the bottom was brown but not burned. After a minute flipped it from the skillet onto a plate. He ate the pan bread with margarine.

He went back to his room and put on a jacket and pants from a thrift store. He had a good suit but he never wore it to work: he did not want to look like a jerk and he had to keep it clean for interviews. Dressed, he went back to the kitchen and made a cheese and cabbage sandwich for lunch. He put it in his backpack and started to work.

He could have taken a bus, subway, or cab, but he did not make much money and liked the exercise of walking. He had three choices for the first leg of the journey uptown. He could walk along Allen Street, which was usually quiet but did involve walking by a housing project which could mean a hassle. Christie Street he never really considered: junkies and prostitutes were there round the clock. The Bowery would mean being hit up for spare change about a dozen times, though it was no problem once he got north of Houston Street. He decided to risk Allen Street: it was usually safe in the morning, and then he could come back on The Bowery in the evening.

The skinny hispanic prostitute was at the corner and he said good morning. He wanted to talk with her but was shy and did not have any money. He knew that Snark would not let her stay with them and that he could not afford to rent an apartment of his own. He was sad that she had to stand waiting for some trucker or businessman to come by. He worried that she would have syphilis. He told himself he would take her out when he had some money.

There were a few people hanging out at the project but they were not out on the sidewalk. First Avenue had lots of people on it, going to work, getting breakfast. They were not objects of curiosity for him, as they might be on a leisurely walk: they were obstacles between him and work. New Yorkers walk fast, but he was eating up sidewalk faster than most joggers would. At Saint Mark's place he turned left, East, because he liked walking up Third Avenue or Lexington or Park. He let the necessity of waiting on stoplights and traffic steer him to Park Avenue. He could see the Pan Am Building when he looked up, but he concentrated on passing the slow moving crowds. He was in a deep canyon now, filled with impatient cabs and deadly exhaust gasses.

As he neared the Pan Am building it became difficult to move faster than the crowd; there were not enough openings. He had to wait his turn to enter the doors of Grand Central station, dodge across its great lobby, and wait again to get a turn on the escalator. At least he did not have to sardine himself into an elevator: his work place was on the mezzanine.

8:57. He was on time. Usually he was late to one degree or another. He greeted his fellow workers: Michael and Lena. Fred would be late, as would their supervisor, Mary Lou. The office consisted of three rooms: one full of files, one with a table where they reviewed documents, and one occupied by the xerox machine. Jack could never face a xerox machine early in the morning, so he sat down at the table and prepared to work by chatting with Michael.

"Do anything last night?" asked Jack.

"Don't have the money. I listened to music. Did you go to the Mudd Club?"

"No, it's such a bore. I only go there with friends who want to get in free. I went to A7 for about an hour."

"A7? How can you stand punk music?"

"The people are nice. There aren't too many rich assholes there. New wave is OK to listen to, but punks are alive."

"I heard people get in fights there. What's the point of that."

"I don't go much, but I haven't seen a fight, just slam dancing."

"Not my idea of fun. Do you get in free?"

"Rockschool doesn't want anything to do with them. But it was only $2."

"High guys." It was Mary Lou. She was a law school graduate but had not found a job and was waiting for her New York Bar results, so she was passing time supervising temps for the paralegal agency. Her main pastime was flirting with the men, who were all a decade younger than her, and accusing them of being gay when they did not respond. She had an Wasp American apple pie of a face, but was easygoing enough.

Jack read. Fred came in and started xeroxing with Lena. They would switch off later. They were all paralegals working for Career Blazers temporary services. They were paid $5.50 an hour. The agency charged Upper, Class, & Twits $15 an hour for their services. The law firm charged their clients, Universalmega Press, UP, $30 an hour. Mary Lou, of course was more. So the meter was ticking at $170 an hour for the five of them. That was cheap: having five associate lawyers do it would have cost three times as much and they would have done a worse job.

UP was being sued by its female reporters for alleged sexual bias in making promotions. The paralegals' job was going through the personnel files marking every piece of paper that might relate to the case. Later the lawyers would decide which evidence to build their case on. Somewhere another law firm, representing the plaintiffs, was going through the same documents, picking out the same documents, and selecting from them the documents that they hoped would prove discrimination.

Mainly it was boring to read. The typical story was that someone aspired to be a world renowned journalist. They went to journalism school and then covered fires and press conferences for a while. They wrote fast and well and landed a job with the UP, and then never left the town they were in.

Some people actually did get sent overseas or to Washington D.C. to cover the big news. Beginning in the 1960's, quite a few were sent to South Vietnam. Many did not like what they saw, and sent back very accurate descriptions of what was going on. That was fine: if something made America or the Pentagon look bad it was kicked upstairs to Terry Galahad, and it never went out on the wire to all the local papers that rely on UP for their international news. Even if some things did go out, they were rarely printed by the local papers. Occasionally one of the reporters would complain. "I think the American people should know that American troops are raping women and burning villages... I want to know why my story did not go out on the wire." Often the reporter did not know that other reporters had already fought the same fight. The reply could be condensed to "We welcome your reports but cannot send unverified information out on the wire. If you want you can go back to reporting on fires and tornados in Des Moines." Once, only once that Jack and his friends saw, a reporter whose story had been rejected by UP sold it to a French paper. It was then republished in Le Monde and in England's major dailies, and only weeks after it was written did it appear in the New York Times. It never was seen by most U.S. newspaper readers.

Jack was so depressed by the reactionary climate of the late 1970's that he did not bother to xerox the documents showing how news is censored in the U.S. Later he would regret missing the opportunity. He was glad, however, that he had not wasted time becoming a journalist.

A couple of years later Jack landed inside a bigger mess. There are lots of law firms in the United States, and Smiles, Fetters & Gruesome, as it is known in the trade, is no better or worse than any of them. It could have been in any city of over 100,000 souls, but by chance it is in Seattle. As in all things Jack came to be employed by the firm partly by design and partly by chance, and mostly out of desperation. He did not want a job, he had more than enough to do, and his actions were constructive. However, he was not being paid for them. He was living in a tiny room with his girlfriend, who was not really supporting him. They were both at the mercy of the owner of the house, who supported their cause and let them stay for free.

He did not learn until a year and a half later, but Smiles, Fetters was desperate too. So desperate they put an ad in the Seattle Times for a legal assistant. They wanted someone with experience with computerized litigation, so they pulled his resume out of the four hundred they received.

He scoured the second-hand stores for the best $7 suit he could find. He was not sure which resume he had sent them so he took copies of both his paralegal resumes, hoping to keep the story straight. As soon as he saw the personnel manager, an old skinny woman with a waspy face, he asked her which ad had been theirs, and then he was able to fill out the application form she gave him with lies that matched the ones they already had. Well, not lies: exaggerations.

For the first time in his life he really wanted a job: he had a good use for the money. There had been times in the past when he had been broke, hungry and indebted and would still tell the truth in a job interview. This time he was totally sincere when he said he wanted the job, and otherwise lied through his teeth.

Two days later the personnel manager called him and invited him to a second interview. It would be with the paralegals and lawyers he would be working with. So he went for a second time into the huge black tomb that then dominated the city skyline and ascended to the heights where one could sense one owned or at least ran an entire city. The view was impressive: to the north lay most of downtown, then the Space Needle, then the canal and suburbs. To the East was First Hill, then Lake Washington, then the Cascade Mountains. Mount Rainier rose over the horizon to the south, and to the west were first the docks, then Puget Sound, and finally the snow capped Olympic Mountains. He was interviewed by three paralegals, one man and two women; all were attractive people of about his age. He was to take the place of the man, who was leaving to try to become a rock star. With these people he felt he could be a bit lively, but mainly he gave the Right Answers.

He then met the lawyer he would work with, and he seemed rather nice, for a lawyer. Jack could tell the lawyer liked him, and he knew that even when he wasn't trying to he sometimes got jobs because people liked him. He was almost beginning to look forward to the job: it certainly would be easier than what he was doing.

He was an anti-war organizer. A few months earlier the U.S. had begun installing Pershing Missiles in western Europe despite a major insurrection in West Germany. He had been there and seen the resistance with his own eyes or heard about it from participants: the riots at Bremerhaven, Hamburg, Bonn, Mutlagen, and Frankfort and the violent police attacks on peaceful protestors in a dozen cities. Scarier than the German Reality had been coming back to the U.S. and learning that virtually no one in the U.S. knew what had happened. CBS, NBC, and ABC had shown protestors lighting candles, praying and holding hands, and men debating in Parliament. He had seen their cameras filming the riots. It was indeed 1984 and he thought we would be lucky to see 1985.

So he pretty much knew he had the job. The bait had been perfect: some experience in writing resumes, blue eyes, TV diction, a haircut and a carefully selected $7 suit. He was asked to come back for one final interview with the lawyer who was head of the team for the WPPSS case, as it was known. They wanted to do the interview during the National Convention of the Democratic Party, but Jack asked them to postpone it to the following Monday. So he saw the American Left sell out and march for Mondale in San Francisco, except for the anarchists, who got creamed by the Police for just trying to gather together to do a bit of educational work about the funny thing of the same corporations funding the democrats as the republicans. The war chest tour, they called it.

Smiles, Fetters was not the premier law firm in Seattle, but, like the other big corporate law firms in the city, it had old and strong ties to money concentrated in the hands of the few families who generally got their way in Seattle. These families had wisely not invested in WPPSS bonds, and therefore there was no conflict of interest in Smiles, Fetters coming to the rescue of the Pacific Northwest. Indeed, even if those families had invested substantially in the bonds it would have been suicidal to demand that they be paid.

Aluminum is not the lightest metal. Hydrogen, helium, lithium, beryllium, boron, carbon, nitrogen, fluorine, neon, sodium, magnesium, aluminum. So goes the periodic table. But the other light metals, lithium, sodium, magnesium and beryllium, react violently with other elements, including air, and boron is relatively rare and not very ductile. Aluminum is one of the commonest metals of the earth's crust and, while inherently reactive, becomes coated with a microscopic coating of aluminum oxide upon exposure to air or water, thus protecting it from further corrosion. However, because of its reactivity, it bonds rather strongly to other elements. It cannot be easily smelted, as iron can. Its efficient production requires electricity. With electricity aluminum is made from its ore as easily as God is said to have made man from clay.

The Cascade Mountains are the remains of the collision of the expanding Pacific ocean floor with the continental crust. The stone thrust up above sea level has been whittled down by millions of years of rain. That rain still falls, mostly in the westernmost of the Cascades near the ocean. As it falls the air dries, so that by the time, going eastward, you reach eastern Washington State you are in a desert that can be farmed only by irrigation. The irrigation requires power, which is furnished by electricity.

The water that does not evaporate or transmogrify into wheat or forest runs downhill until it reaches the Pacific Ocean. Long before the first white settlers had invaded the Oregon Country other Europeans had discovered that such falling water could be made to do mechanical work by turning wheels. Before there were as many as a million people living in the American section of the Oregon Territory other men had advanced in their understanding of electricity to the point where they could make the falling water turn a dynamo that produced electricity.

Electricity was cheap before 1980 in the States of Washington and Oregon. All one had to do was build a dam, put a dynamo in it, and run a wire to wherever you wanted the electricity. Before 1920 mostly the dams were small and could be built by private enterprise or the towns and cities that needed them. However, much of the water continued to run down to the sea unimpeded through the Columbia River. A dam across the Columbia would be a truly major undertaking, and a risky one in that it might produce so much electricity that no one would want it all. The Depression had struck by the time this was a consideration. So the federal government built the dam and established an agency, the Bonneville Power Administration, to oversee the transmission and sale of electricity.

The Boeing Company made quite a few airplanes for the Federal Government during the first world war. They were made mostly out of wood and steel. By the time the Bonneville dam was completed aluminum had become the standard material for making airplanes. It was also becoming a generally useful substance, and despite the Depression a group of investors with enough capital who could hire the right expertise and get the raw materials cheap enough could figure to make a good profit. There are three main raw materials necessary to make aluminum: that type of clay known as bauxite, electricity, and labor. Bauxite could be mined cheaply and then transported by barge to almost anywhere in the world. Cheap labor was in no great shortage, between the crushing of the Wobblies and the Depression. The key ingredient was electricity, and it was made as cheaply by the weather and mountains and Columbia River and Federal government as anywhere in the world. So the aluminum industry came to the Pacific Northwest in a big way. They made a handsome profit, too, because even after World War II there was not only the Cold War but the spectacular growth of the airline industry.

Everything was going fine until sometime in the early sixties when some engineer or bureaucrat or economist noted that if the demand for electricity continued to climb at the rate it was climbing soon there would not be anyplace left to build any dams that were worth building. In other words, sometime in the late 1970's, the region would run short of electricity. No one wanted this to happen. The area was not crowded; less people lived in all of two enormous states than lived in Brooklyn.

Fortunately, it was already known that falling water was not the only source of electricity; it was merely the cheapest source. Most parts of the United States got their electricity by burning coal or petroleum, which were not as inexpensive as Pacific Northwest running water, but were cheap. So if new plants were built the costs would be averaged in with the virtually free hydroelectricity, and no one was apt to complain.

Only the Federal Government wanted to build nuclear plants. It is not entirely clear why, probably because there were different reasons. Maybe one was guilt about Hiroshima and Nagasaki. Certainly one was the need to create more plutonium to either prevent future Hiroshimas or cause them, depending on how you looked at the continuing arms race. Probably they really believed that, once they got the technology down, nuclear power would be, if not too cheap to meter, at least cheaper than coal or gas produced electricity.

But who would build the nuclear plants? Because the projections showed that towards the end of the 1970's one new nuclear plant would need to be built every two years. And each of the new plants would be very, very expensive, the same, at least, as building a huge dam. And worse, it was known that it took about 8 years from the conception of a nuclear plant until the time it produced electricity. All that time there would be money tied up in the plant, and no revenue would come in until the electricity began to flow.

The aluminum companies needed the electricity, but they knew it would be expensive stuff, and they wanted the ordinary people to buy the expensive stuff while they continued to get the hydropower. In fact the various cities thought the same way. They also did not want to raise taxes to pay for the plants, especially since then there were bound to be a few ornery citizens who would file lawsuits to block the plants, figuring there was no shortage of wood about to burn and keep warm with. So everyone figured the Federal Government would do it, meaning BPA, since it was their idea anyway.

But BPA did not have the statutory authority to build nuclear power plants. In fact, they did not build the dams: the Corp of Engineers did, and ran them too. BPA built transmission lines and sold the electricity. The Vietnam War was on, and the Great Society, and there was no interest in Congress in getting directly into the nuclear power plant business.

BPA whipped up a holy terror of fear of impending brownouts in the Pacific Northwest. And somewhere some bureaucrat or lawyer found the loophole that saved the situation. A loophole big enough to drive a few nuclear power plants through. It was known as the Washington Public Power Supply System (WPPSS). No one back then referred to it as Whoops.

WPPSS, which had never built anything much larger than a small dam, had the authority to build nuclear power plants. But not only did its customers, which were in rural Washington, not need expensive electricity, but they did not really need much more electricity at all. However, they did not really know much about it. WPPSS and Bonneville did almost everything for them. If something was needed BPA would tell them, and the local government would pass it without discussion because they did not understand it anyway.

So bonds were sold for three nuclear power plants, WPPSS 1,2, and 3. The bonds were backed by WPPSS and in turn by the municipalities and coops and rural electric authorities that were WPPSS's and Bonneville's customers. Bonneville would buy all the electricity and blend the nuclear electricity in with the hydropower and sell it to whoever needed it. Better still, BPA would pay for the power even if it were not being produced, which meant that WPPSS would be able to pay off the bonds even if construction were delayed.

Around the country bond brokers sold the bonds to people who had made so much money that they needed tax free and risk free income. True, some middle class people bought a few thousand dollars worth of the bonds, and some depended on these to remain in the middle class upon retirement. But mostly big money bought them, including insurance companies and trust funds.

Sites were found and contractors hired and machinery arrived and cleared the sights and designers began designing the plants and the plants began to be built. But time crept forward and consumption of electricity increased each year and by the time those first three plants were finished they would be needing one new nuclear plant a year. Only the federal government did not like BPA promising to buy power that might not be delivered on time, because then

BPA would have to borrow money from the Federal Government and the national debt was already skyrocketing.

So WPPSS #4 and WPPSS #5 bonds were sold without the buy back guarantee of BPA. Instead they were backed by the local governments and electric authorities that BPA had told would need the electricity. They would pay off the bonds come hell or high water, according to contracts they signed. And they weren't worried, not yet, because BPA told them that the electricity would be needed, that the problem was that even with all five power plants built there would be a shortage of electricity. So local elected officials spent an hour discussing if the town should buy a new pickup truck and what kind, and three hours discussing whether to put a stoplight or just a stop sign at the new intersection with Main Street, and approved the contracts obligating them for tens or even hundreds of millions of dollars worth of bonds with seldom more than five minutes of discussion.

Some of the brokers who sold the WPPSS 4 and 5 bonds may have forgotten to mention that BPA did not back them as it had those for 1,2,3. But if someone asked they could say they were guaranteed because the electricity was needed and anyway, Moodys had rated them top quality, and there were the high or hellwater clauses.

It was all there, in minute detail, some of it in newspaper stories and just about all of it in hundreds of boxes of documents stored in a room leased just for that purpose by Smiles, Fetters. By the time Jack arrived at Smiles, Fetters the case had already been tried once in state court, and now it was being appealed to a federal court. Millions of documents, everything that had anything to do with the whole mess and quite a bit that did not, from WPPSS, BPA, the cities, towns, and electric authorities, bond rating agencies, underwriters, contractors, the nuclear regulatory commission: all had to be looked at, because blame would be weighed by details, by a judge and jury that would know as little about nuclear power, bond markets, and electricity forecasting as the lawyers who were defending the myriad interests in the case.

He started reading documents and trying to figure out what was going on. Fortunately he was a paralegal and that gave the law firm's clients considerable advantage over the Wall Street interests. Because Merrill Lynch et al. were not about to risk blowing a multi-billion dollar lawsuit by having their lawyers allow mere paralegals to read through these millions of documents. No, real attorneys were needed. But no real attorney would want to do that, so associate attorneys, a year or two out of lawschool, were assigned to it.

So not only did they not know very much about The Law, but they knew next to nothing about anything else. They had gone from toddlerhood through lawschool with hardly a glance at reality, excepting perhaps the bowdlerized histories of the American school system. They had no training in science; they did not know how a transistor radio worked, much less a nuclear power plant. They did not know the reality of constructing a building; they were not apt to notice a peculiar work order for welds or extra piping. Perhaps, since they were from professional or wealthy families or they would never gotten to be an associate at a top corporate law firm, they understood something about municipal bonds besides that you do not have to pay taxes on the interest from them. But probably not.

Maybe they knew about elasticity of demand, even if they had never taken an economics course. Because that was the guilty party, pure and simple. Excluding yuppies, when something costs more, less of it will be bought. So when the price of electricity starts going up, even people in the Pacific Northwest, who were accustomed to not turning off light bulbs because their monthly electricity bills were so low either way, would begin to turn off unnecessary light bulbs and conserve energy.

By the time they finally got one of those nuclear power plants started no one wanted the electricity. Because they had long been paying off the bonds, and electricity rates had risen, and people started conserving energy.

By the time Jack finished snooping around those documents he was glad they had only managed to start one nuclear plant. He had been a carpenter and worked on a concrete pour and done some plumbing and electrical work and could both program a computer and take it apart and put it back together; he had lived with the poor and the rich and the middle class and seen how the economy works in reality as well as in the Wall Street Journal; he had run a small business, he had examined statistics to sort out deception and argued with scientists and politicians and realized he was wrong enough times to learn a few things. And since he already knew basic engineering physics and quantum physics and human nature and had even once worked for a government bureaucracy, the documents served as a sort of graduate course in nuclear power plant design, construction, and finance.

If you live near a nuclear power plant you live near a nuclear bomb that is barely kept under control even presuming things are going perfectly right. It is run on the principle that, if it were a gasoline powered automobile, instead of having a tank of highly explosive gasoline from which a bit is siphoned at a time to be exploded in the cylinders of an engine, the entire tank of gas is heated almost to the point where it will explode and then the heat produced is siphoned off just fast enough to keep it from exploding.

It is not built like a car or a house. Or rather it is built like cars were built when a man would build an engine and buy some gears and contrive to connect the engine to the wheels of a carriage meant to be pulled by a horse or mule. Because they did not take a design off the shelf and use it to build WPPSS 1. They did not even take the design they drew up for WPPSS 1 and use it to build WPPSS 2, perhaps with some changes they had made after learning from their mistakes. They did not even design WPPSS 1 before they started building it. They designed part of WPPSS 1, the foundation at least, and while that was being built they designed the buildings and reactor and cooling system and turbines, only not all at once, but trying to keep one step ahead of the workers, which you would think would be easy since the work was always behind schedule, and often not succeeding even in that. And frequently, having gotten to part #1,122,987 and designed it, they would realize that the structure erected to hold it was too big or small or short or fat and some or all of that structure would have to be torn down and then built again.

The men who built it were good men, as men go, but their bosses needed to make a profit and some of them might fairly be said to be greedy. So it was a hurrying sort of slowness that was building the plants: when the design was ready and the materials had arrived and the prior work that needed to be done was done, then the work was done as quickly as was possible, which often enough bordered on carelessness. Sometimes a Nuclear Regulatory Commission man would come around and look at work and say it had to be done over, but mostly the sloppy work was not obvious. Even a practiced eye may not know that a weld that looks good on the outside is strained on the inside, and that one day that weld is going to give and that barely restrained explosion is no longer going to be barely restrained. There are millions of welds in a nuke plant.

So eventually some of the contractors were sued, but you could not really blame it on them. Nor could you blame it on the designers, because they would just as soon have done the whole design before the work was begun. A lot of people blamed the mess on BPA, but that was not just because BPA had undertaken to oversee construction only to protect the federal interest; it was because of the elasticity of demand, which nobody but BPA could have been expected to think of. Only they were not BPA's plants, and BPA had never built, even through obfuscation, a nuclear plant, so even they could not be expected to know about the cost overruns. The original estimates were off by a factor of five, more or less.

The bonds on WPPSS 4 and 5 defaulted. It was not even just the delays and elasticity and Three Mile

Island. It was interest rates. Most people do not realize the pernicious nature of compound interest. Suppose money has to be borrowed for 8 years before electricity is sold and even a cent of it is paid back, and supposing it can be borrowed, because the dividends will be tax free, at the reasonable rate of 7% per years. Get out your calculator and multiply 100 by .07 and add that back to the 100 and multiply again and do that 8 times. You get 171.82 that is owed by the time you can start to pay. Only now 7% per year on that $171 is $12, without even beginning to pay back all that expanded principle.

Now suppose it has been ten years and still no electricity can be produced and you are selling bonds just to pay the interest that began to come due after eight years. And suppose people are beginning to worry about your bonds and see them as a risk and want an extra percentage point of interest in order to buy your bonds. And suppose there is a new Chairman of the Federal Reserve Board who is worried about inflation and restricts the money supply and all the sudden you have to pay 14% per year to sell bonds. And you realize about that same time that a plant that was supposed to cost $600,000,000 to build is going to cost three billion dollars not counting financing. Calculate what 14% of that is compounded over a few years. And you would stop building those plants too, elasticity or no elasticity.

So now the hemorrhage on your almost tame Nagasaki is staunched and all you have to do is pay off the bonds you have already sold. Which means all you have to do is double or triple your electricity rates, which after all were the lowest in the nation and even after doubling or tripling will be not much above the national average.

Supposing you are growing potatoes or wheat on a few hundred acres of irrigated land out in eastern Washington and you buy your electricity from a Coop that buys it from BPA. You require several thousands of dollars a year to buy electricity to pump that water and had figured it was OK because you got it back in crops more or less, which is to say that despite the mortgage and the loans on farm equipment and an occasional bad crop you have ten or twenty thousand dollars a year left over to spend on your family. And now the newspapers are saying your costs are going to go up say $6000 a year, and you know damn well the prices of crops are not going up. What would you do?

They defaulted on those bonds. The eastern establishment newspapers started talking about school teachers who had bought a few bonds for their retirement; how could you? Never mind that most of the tax free bonds were bought by rich people and their corporate masks to avoid having to help pay for roads, schools, aircraft carriers, MX missiles and other necessities of modern society.

The problem was that those bondholders were not going to get their money anyway, unless the federal government bailed them out. Because suppose they honored, all those people in the Pacific Northwest, their commitments. First a whole bunch of farmers and small industries that were heavily dependent on electricity would go under. Then some of the people who sold cars and groceries to those people would to under. Then maybe 5% of the electrical demand would be gone, but the bonds would still have to be paid for, so electric rates would go up another 5%. Then there would be more conservation and more farmers going under and more factories closing. And consumption would be down another 10% and rates up another 10% even just from millions of people turning off light bulbs and space heaters. And it would not stop. They referred to it as the Death Spiral, because it is one thing to milk a cow, and another to make a couple of gallons of blood pudding out of it every day.

So Seattle's elite was very interested in seeing that those bonds not be paid, because if they were paid Seattle's banks and insurance companies and real estate companies and almost everything but Boeing and the Trident nuclear missile submarine base would go under. And there Jack was, defending some of the people who had defaulted. Of course, they had never figured on the legal fees, which they were paying for through liability insurance, which is not much different than auto-collision insurance: you can never win, because if you are never in an accident you are paying for nothing, but if you are in an accident they raise your rates and get their money back anyway, if you live long enough.

Someone, somewhere was paying $40 an hour for his time, which might seem quite fair, since the other side was paying associate lawyers $80 an hour to do a worse job at the same thing. He was glad to have the job, though he was only getting $7.50 an hour of that $40 an hour for his share. He was not even angry that some bumbling lawyers a few years older than him, were getting not only the $150 an hour they charged the clients, but also $60 of the $80 an hour they charged for the associates work and $30 or so of the $40 an hour they charged for him. There were half a dozen or so paralegals and another half dozen associates working on the case, so the Partners of the firm were doing pretty well off the misery of others.

There were over a dozen law firms involved in the case, and they were loosely grouped into two sides, the defendants and plaintiffs. They shared information, or at least the work of looking at all those documents, with the firms on their side. Once, when Jack was in a room of lawyers and paralegals reviewing boxes of documents, this bleached blond Dorris Day type associate said she did not feel bad taking money from corporate clients, distinguishing them from the non-corporate clients they were supposed to be working for. Because corporations have plenty of money she said. And Jack could not keep his mouth shut. He had kept it shut so long, organizing outside in the streets and being the good quiet worker in the office, and he said:

"Sure like IBM. Plenty of money. Where does it come from? Selling computers to other big corporations that are owned by the same banks and insurance companies anyway. Only how do they make those computers? Paying women in third world countries pennies an hour to look though microscopes and ruin their eyes soldering leads onto integrated circuits. And maybe the women have sisters working in other factories, maybe a textile factory for a dollar a day, and the owners of the textile factory keep track of that daily dollar on an IBM computer in their corporate headquarters in New York City where their young executives work hard and can go out and blow forty dollars in an evening at the Mud Club or even just a French restaurant not counting cocaine."

Which meant his term there was limited. Because word got around and by the time he asked for May 1 off everyone knew why. And one associate, a sharp one or at least one who was not a total idiot and was still diligent, one day was asking him if he had any intention of going to law school. Then he said "Do you know about Dan Dannystone? He was a student at the University of Washington back in the 1960's. He was against the war in Vietnam and went so far as to set off a bomb at the Applied Physics Lab. They caught him and convicted him and he served some time in jail. Then when he got out he went to law school and he was a smart guy and did O.K. Then he passed the bar exam and applied for admission to the bar. And they knew about the bombing conviction and of course would not admit him. The funny thing is how such a smart guy could believe that he could get admitted to the bar after committing a felony."

And Jack said nothing. He did not say "Which is about right, because you did fight in Vietnam and flew a jet and dropped bombs on women and children you could not see, only you were told they were the enemy. People who would not even have known you existed, who held you no grudge. Which is different than killing your wife or a friend in anger or a partner or parent out of greed, which is at least human. But what you did was like breaking into the house of a family you have never met and killing them and not even getting a rise out of it or bothering to take anything valuable from them. So the Bar Association had no problem with your ethics, because you understand lawyer ethics, it is simply a matter of following orders."

They were trying to help him, straighten him out. He was smart and all he had to do was go to law school and then sign up as an associate and then in six years he could be like them, buy a yacht and a million dollar home and a manikin wife. Or even just work steadily as a paralegal and save up a down payment for a home and then save up a down payment to buy a second home and rent it out and then have both mortgages paid off after ten years and retire if he wanted to.

Which was too bad, because he actually liked going in there, saying hello to the receptionist, and walking back to his tiny windowless office. He would decide what had to be done that day and maybe even decide to do it. A bookshelf held bound copies of the important documents he had put together, along with memos in the front explicating what the documents proved. Usually he did not even have to spend that much time in the office, because to use a computer he had to go to another room, and to look at the documents, of which there was a never ending supply, he usually went over to another office building. It was easy compared to political organizing, to petting and cajoling egos, to trying to make reality something other than a fog for the people he met, to persuading (though himself unconvinced) that people could do things that would reverse the forces pushing the world towards war and other forms of mass suicide. It was almost like sleep with pleasant dreams, walking into the office, chatting a bit with other paralegals and legal secretaries and messengers, skimming through the documents and occasionally seizing a prize one and adding it to his trophies. Or summarizing a deposition, noting carefully the personalities behind the techniques of the lawyers, watching the guilty and incompetent and greedy squirm or blandly pretend that they had waltzed through their high-paid jobs as if on opium and now could not only not remember a thing they had done but did not recognize letters and memos that they had signed and hence presumably written.

Few people see the value of honesty. Even those that do are usually lost in the confusion: the world creates its own illusions, and power crazed people find it useful to multiply them. Most people find it convenient to believe what their parents, families, and friends believe: Jews beget Jews, Buddhists beget Buddhists, Christians beget Christians. The truth is likely to be found where such systems of propagation clash: seaports, border towns, and the centers of great empires. If everyone in a community believes in heaven the fact that no one has seen it is no cause for concern, but the appearance of one person who denies it can provoke great crisis.

Even the pursuit of truth can become a vehicle for illusion. Jack, by the time he arrived in Seattle, knew enough to know that getting facts straight was crucial to accomplishing his goal: preventing nuclear war. He wanted to form an army to overthrow the government. He did not want the government replaced by a new, better one: governments, at best, are machines waiting to be taken over by a Stalin, Hitler, Rockefeller, or Kennedy. He was open to different opinions: he did not think it was impossible for nonviolent struggle to achieve the goal, or even for electoral politics to; that was just highly unlikely.

He checked out as many groups as he could; most were Leninist. There was the Red Planet group, which was advocating direct action; the Freedom Socialist Party (FSP), which was led by women and generated an emotional, revivalist type atmosphere while talking about an electable socialist party; the Marxist-Leninist Party, which consisted of hard core dogmatic Leninist jargon slingers who professed that Albania was the only true workers' paradise; Line of March, which seemed the most moderate, intent on working with Jesse Jackson; the African Peoples Socialist Party (APSP), which was unfriendly to white men; the Socialist Worker's Party (SWP), which appeared union oriented and overly cautious; and, of course, the good old Communist Party, U.S.A. (CPUSA), which operated in the Peace Movement by painting the Soviet Union as Utopia and attacking anyone who criticized it.

Then there was the Revolutionary Communist Party, always referred to as the RCP. Several things made this group attractive to Jack. They openly advocated armed revolution. They spent a lot of time in the streets and at political events selling their newspaper, the Revolutionary Worker. And the people assigned to work in the Peace movement included two very intelligent women, Belinda and Blade.

He was first approached by Lili. Jack was about to give a lecture at the old firehouse on Capitol Hill that had been converted into a community center. The lecture was on the Federal Reserve System and how it was designed to give money to banks and corporations, hundreds of billions of dollars every year, without anyone knowing it. Lili was selling a newspaper, the Revolutionary Worker, which had an article in it that looked interesting, and she gave it to him for a quarter dollar when he pleaded poverty. He was disappointed when she did not stay for his lecture.

He was checking things out. He had signed on as Business Manager of Northwest Nuclear Xchange, first as a volunteer and then as a full time staff person at $400 a month. He was renting a room in a house from two mindless cleanliness fascists at $130 a month and did not have a car, so he did not feel impoverished. He was most interested in Direct Action, but also felt the situation called for armed rebellion, so he was looking for individuals and organizations that worked along those lines. He thought of himself as an anarchist, but the anarchists he had met were all either pacifists or armchair types. There was not much around, but he heard that a group called Armistice had organized massive civil disobediences a couple of years earlier at the new Trident nuclear submarine base at Bangor, a stone's throw away from Seattle.

So he called them, and they did not call him back. He went to their office and talked to their staff person, who was not eager to talk about civil disobedience, and never heard from them. Finally he went to a combined potluck/lecture. No one much talked to him during the potluck, though he attempted to initiate a few conversations. There were about thirty people for the lecture, which was by Lila from Evergreen University in Olympia, and she was devastatingly pretty (Jack was sleeping with no one at that point and hence lusted after virtually every woman he met) but not particularly inspiring. When she was finished the woman from Armistice asked if there were questions and only one woman raised her hand.

"I think," the woman said "that there really is no way of convincing the Imperialists to give up their objective of world conquest when that is precisely what their economies depend on, and that given that what we should be organizing for is armed revolution. That means not allowing the peace movement to be coopted into electoral politics..."

Both Rosemary and Lila interrupted Belinda. "I would be happy to answer a question," said Lila, "but I don't see the point of advocating armed revolution in a forum like this. Right now the problem is convincing people that the problem exists."

Steve of Red Planet, his hand up but without waiting to be called on, said "I think she should be allowed to speak if this is going to be an open discussion."

Rosemary was not about to allow that. "We invited Lila here to present her viewpoint to Armistice members. We have a limited amount of time and I think it is only fair that Armistice members have a chance to hear what Lila has to say. If there is time after the question and answer session we can have a general discussion."

So there was not a general discussion, and after the meeting Belinda ran for the door, only to whip out her stack of RW's and try to sell them to each person who came out. Meanwhile Jack tried to engage her in a conversation about armed revolution. Finally, when everyone else had left, she gave him a newspaper and took his phone number. All the while he was studying her face, which he liked: it was a girl version of his friend Snark's face at Rockschool. He lusted after her, and wished she had been more friendly.

Once she found out he was a staff person on a newspaper with a circulation of 10,000 she started coming by Nuclear Xchange to see him once a week. She would tell him about the other political groups in Seattle and why they did what they did, but mainly she would talk about current events as reported in the Revolutionary Worker. Much of the interpretation he agreed with as he heard it: he knew how vicious and calculating America and the USSR's rulers were. He also agreed that the result would be nuclear war, and that the only hope for stopping it was armed revolution. He thought that his only difference with the RCP was that, since he was an anarchist, he believed people could organize themselves without a government. The RCP said that things were fine in Russia until Stalin died; Jack was not sure why people who could be so otherwise astute would believe such a whopper.

It was less than a year and a half later that Jack found himself sitting in a meeting watching a year of his life's work threatening to crumble into nothing.

"You're just trying to hide the fact that you don't believe World War is a possibility," Lili was saying in a high-pitched, emotionally strained voice.

"You're trying to impose your ideology on everyone, and no one wants to join the coalition because they know how manipulative the RCP is."

"Lili" said Jack, "they aren't saying there isn't a danger of nuclear war. They are saying there are other issues that are important and that will attract more people to this. When we met in San Francisco we decided that No Business As Usual could be used as a name by any group that was in general agreement with the Statement, and that groups could do autonomous actions or work together as they like. If the anarchists want to do a separate action, then they are going to do it."

"They can't call it NBAU and they are objectively aiding the imperialists," Lili screeched, and the argument went on, and the anarchists walked out.

The next evening Blade, Jack's girlfriend and cell leader, gave him a big lecture about party members not disagreeing with each other in public, and how Lili was right, and he was wrong for capitulating to the anarchists. He explained to her that she was wrong, that Lili was wrong in attacking the anarchists, and that if she could not understand that they would have to appeal to a higher level of the party.

Up until then he had never had reason to find out how democratic centralism worked in the RCP as opposed to in theory. The theory was that a question was debated in the party and a decision reached, if necessary by majority vote. They everyone acted on the majority opinion. If it was wrong, that would come out as a result of acting on it. To Jack this had a great deal of appeal because, trying to work with people in the peace movement, the consensus process always reduced things to the least common denominator, and even then most people went off in their own direction if they did anything at all.

Up until then when he argued with the others in his cell he generally came to the conclusion that they were right, or at least had enough of a grip on reality to make their conclusion worth trying out. So he had never worried that they never took a vote on anything and that directives came down from the mysterious party bureaucracy. Now he found out being in strong disagreement with his cell leader meant that he was also in disagreement with her superior who would decide the dispute, and so on all the way to the central committee and the Leader, Baba Vakian himself. He thought that he might have a chance if he could argue his case with ordinary party members, but he had no way to talk to them or to force a vote on the question. His eyes were opened a bit: there was no democracy in the RCP, just centralism.

He might have left the party right then, but it turned out that there were divisions in the leadership. A party member in San Francisco who was the NBAU staff person confirmed for Jack that he was right on the issue of autonomy within NBAU. Jack told his cellmates and the local leaders, and to his amazement they did a 180 degree turn. That was even scarier than having to face a wrong headed bureaucracy: these seemingly brilliant people were not thinking for themselves. But he could continue to be in the party and work on NBAU; he would see about reforming the party soon enough.

As soon as NBAU day was over, an astounding success, the most radical demonstration with the most massive participation Seattle had seen since the end of the Vietnam War, Jack was called in by Blade's superior, Labryth, and accused of breaking party discipline. Jack argued that he had done the correct thing, that he would do it again, and that he would appeal the whole thing to the Central Committee if he had to. If the party wanted to overthrow the government and put the workers in power it had to have people in it who could think and act, not a bunch of robots.

Since he moved out of his apartment with Blade his only contact with her was to be harped at. Cell meetings were held for the sole purpose of wearing him down, making him toe the party line. Only he was right, he could demonstrate he was right by pointing to facts and using reason, and the other cell mates began to waiver.

Then he went to yet another cell meeting and it began with Blade accusing him of lacking in "proletarian spirit" because he had not bothered to carry out some of the party's assignments. He walked out of the meeting and, when she came by his apartment, he told her he resigned.

A week or so later Blade asked him to meet with her and a local party leader. They met in a bar, and had hardly sat down when Slacmaster got down to business:

"We believe that the pattern of activity you've engaged in lately is indicative of police activities."

Jack considered throwing beer in the asshole's face, but instead got up and walked out.

Chapter 7

STREET FIGHT

"Two streets cross in Hamburg. Perhaps if I had a map I could identify them, but probably not. I could get back to the general area. Probably someone else who was there at that particular intersection of time and drama had a better reason to know and remembers the names.

I don't even remember how we got there. I might as well have been a private at Verdun for all I knew. I trusted the woman who was shepherding us, and she trusted the people who were shepherding her. I could not speak German and neither could she, but most of the Germans could get by in English. I had looked at the map that had been handed out. I had the map in my pocket and knew the name of the streets we were on.

We were where it was going to be relatively safe, with some pacifists and some Greens. Boring. I wanted to be with the Autonomen and Anarcho--Communists; the fighting would be guaranteed. The ground rules were clear and I accepted them. But my Shepherd valued our hides and did not want us hurt or arrested. We were guests from America, we did not know our way around, we were not trained or equipped as fighters.

There was a barricade up of sorts. It was symbolic: it would stop nothing. Some garbage and some broken bottles and planks. The polizei in their green riot gear were waiting patiently down the street. Safe. Too safe: there were a dozen ways the Springer trucks could get out. Only one had to be opened, and it did not look to be this one.

Mostly people were milling around, but about forty were sitting in the middle of the intersection dressed in raincoats. I wondered why they were wearing raincoats; it was cold, but not cloudy. Time passed; I chatted with my fellow Americans and several Germans who wanted to try their English. No one expected much. There had been a hundred thousand people at the rally earlier that day; there were over ten thousand blocking the streets now. The police would not attack that many people; the politicians would not want to face the heat.

Finally word came by a messenger on a bicycle. The police had attacked where the autonomen were assembled. That was all; no details.

Now there was an influx of people, people who had retreated two intersections over when the police attacked. Our group of seven americans hung closer together now. Our policemen were still waiting down the street, but now people were yelling at them. More bottles were dug out of a dumpster and thrown between us and the police.

The water cannon, essentially a big truck, came up slowly behind a wall of policemen from the street to our left. A policeman was speaking over a loudspeaker, telling us to go home. Pershing II and Cruise missiles in these people's backyards, World War III on the horizon, and maybe a few people went home at that point, but I did not notice any.

Our shepherd pulled us back from the edge of the crowd. I was pretty pissed that this woman was so unprepared to share the risk that I paired off with Watt. He was the only other anarcho- communist in our group. Suddenly there was water in the air: the water cannon was spraying the crowd.

The crowd moved around, avoiding the stream of water. Finally the muzzle of the gun settled on the pacifists. I would not have taken it: I was cold enough, I did not want to be clobbered by ice cold water. They sat there. All I could do for a minute was cry.

Someone threw a rock at the police who were guarding the water cannon. A bottle flew. People were yelling. A dozen policemen hurled themselves at the crowd, but the people opened up around them without leaving. I found there was a loose rock, a piece of cement sidewalk, under a bush off to the side of the street. It was too heavy to throw at the police, but I threw it anyway; it bounced on the ground a couple of times and the police dodged it. My friends had disappeared except for Watt. The pacifists were being clubbed and dragged away.

Suddenly, while I was looking for something else to throw, an army of policemen solid across the street and three deep charged us. Now the crowd ran down the street, but not fast enough, and rather than be caught on its edge I jumped through bushes that marked off the lot of a building. A policeman grabbed me but I kept running even as I slashed backwards with my arm. I was free and ran into an alley. The policeman did not pursue: separated from his fellows he might get beaten to pulp.

Working my way back to the people I found they were standing their ground now. People were digging up cobblestones to throw, but they were too heavy here and served only to keep the police from getting too close. I wondered what was happening to the pacifists, who were now deep inside police lines.

To my surprise I ran into Watt. The rest of our contingent had disappeared, presumably on a rapid retreat to safety. We chatted. Watt was actually handing out our "World Without Imperialism" flier to people. We stayed towards the back of the crowd now: when the police attacked we retreated, when the crowd regrouped we advanced with it. There were no stones being thrown now, just a crowd that did not want to go home.

We decided to see if we could find the autonomen. The street seemed very wide: we walked in the center, there were no cars moving. Lots of people were wandering about, tall blonde Germans in black leather jackets, people with kafiyas covering their faces, people in ski masks, ordinary street clothes, or raincoats. The police moved only in groups; for some reason they did not try to surround the whole area and scoop everyone up. They would not have room for all the people in their jails. The intersection the autonomen were to have defended was empty except for a few dozen police standing guard; the autonomen prefer moving battles. At a construction project there was a cordon of police; we realized that this was the project from which people had hoped to get material for the barricades.

A gang of green-shirted riot police marched down the street, clubbing those who would not disperse but not trying to arrest them. They just moved the crowd around; they stuck together, not wanting to see what the crowd might do to a few isolated pigs.

So much for the Springer Blockade. The tabloid, complete with lies, scant news coverage, pornography, and rightwing editorials would be on the stands as usual the next day. Watt and I made our way carefully to a subway and back to the slum where we were staying.

The fact that Watt was willing to throw stones at the police when the Bolsheviks in our contingent ran yellow did not win him any points with them. The ground rules the Reds made were that criticizing Anarchists was OK, but criticizing the Reds was sewing disunity when all efforts should be directed at discrediting the State. Jack was immune partly because he was naive enough to not know what the Reds were up to, partly because his girlfriend was a Red, and mainly because he was the only "legitimate" representative of the peace movement in the U.S. in the group. He even helped kick Watt out of the contingent soon afterwards, something he regretted as he did it and did not fully comprehend until he was ousted from SNAG back in Seattle over a year later on the grounds that he belonged to the RCP; the people who organized his expulsion were leninists of another persuasion.

An ordinary day in Germany during the hot autumn was not nearly so exciting. They usually stayed in anarchist squats; the Reds did not seem to have any problem accepting charity from anarchists. They did not have any money, generally speaking; most of their group had been lucky to get enough money to come over. It would be bitter cold in the morning; only the body warmth of a dozen or two people sleeping together kept it from being as cold as outdoors. Sergeant Rick would wake everyone up in the morning, especially those who were scheduled to catch trains to attend meetings in other towns. Most of them tried to hide in their sleeping bags, often already wearing their jackets trying to keep warm. Rick was a Red; they know how to get things done, in a fashion.

Breakfast was almost always bread and margarine; when they had arrived there had been jam, milk, coffee, and peanut butter as well. Sometimes there was fruit, if a donation had come in. After breakfast those of them who remained behind would go to their rendezvous with their leaders, who had warm accommodations furnished by the Turkish communists. They would be informed of what happened the previous day and would make suggestions about what should be done. If there was a demonstration, they would take out their fliers to hand out or try to talk the organizers into letting them make a statement. They tried to get the media to interview them, which took up much time and almost never resulted in anything happening, largely because their press releases were so obviously radical rhetoric. They would spend a lot of time talking to themselves or to the Turks or occasional Germans who had befriended them. Some of them would try to write new political statements. Often Jack found an excuse to just get away from people and read a book; he felt much of their activity was just spinning their wheels. The only thing that might change people's minds were the fliers they handed out.

Everything possible was being done by West Germany's rulers to thwart the popular will. Everything looked fine in the German Federal Republic, but scratch off the cosmetics and there was nothing but puss and dead bone. Downtown Koln was bright, clean concrete and glass, with luxuries displayed in the windows: a shopper's paradise. 80% of the shoppers, of all West Germans, according to a poll taken a few months before the missiles were ready to be deployed, were against setting up the Pershing and Cruise nuclear missiles on German soil. It is true that a big percentage of these people did not think a great deal about politics, economics, and military strategy; it is also true that a big percentage of the people who did not want the missiles were nationalist Germans who would not have been bothered if they were German rather than American nukes. But most important of all, most of them were used to being sheep: they had never taken any political action in their lives, except perhaps to vote, which requires the intelligence of sheep being fleeced.

The problem for the German godfathers was that they had thought they could put in the missiles without anyone but a small and powerless peace movement noticing. But they had not reckoned with reality. Peace is one thing in abstract: destabilizing, first-strike, American missiles in Germans' backyards is another. There was also the Green Party, which included many disillusioned Stalinists who had seized upon issues such as ecology in order to get a piece of the political pie in their middle age. They were revealed to be great organizers once they started selling peace, the environment, and economic reform instead of Mao, Trotsky, Stalin or similar idiocies.

Instead of talking to each other, the peace activists started talking to other people. People started listening, and deciding yes, enough is enough, these Pershing and Cruise missiles would get them all killed. They began giving money to the peace groups, showing up in larger numbers at rallies and demonstrations, even volunteering and, most important off all, talking to their neighbors and relatives.

Then there were the pitched street battles between the police and the Autonomen, and the enlarging numbers of German youths who dropped out and became punk rockers if not Autonomen.

When the Godfathers suddenly were confronted with thousands of people performing civil disobedience or rioting, tens of thousands showing up at demonstrations, millions voting for Green Party candidates, and polls showing most people moving towards opposition to both the missiles and established foreign and military policy, they realized they had made a mistake. But it was correctable: all they had to do was to get the people who had woken up to go back to sleep. There is a standard way of doing that: it is what political parties, churches, labor unions, and political operatives are for. Only you can't just tell people to go back to sleep; you have to guide them gently back to bed, assuring them they are accomplishing what they set out to do.

Suddenly in early 1983 everyone was for peace and against the Pershing and Cruise Missiles, except the Bad Guys: the Christian Democrats, who just happened to have a majority in parliament. The Churches were against the Missiles, so it was no longer necessary to go and talk to radicals and perhaps be radicalized in order to keep from dying in a nuclear war. You could go to Church sponsored rallies and hear totally bland speakers plead for calm. The Social Democrats, who had ruled Germany most of the years since World War II and who were in the party founded by Karl Marx and Fred Engels, yes, the same Social Democrats who had asked the U.S. government to put in the missiles in the first place, came out against the missiles. So now you did not have to vote Green or associate with Greens to be against the missiles. The labor unions came out against the missiles, which was extra important, because now factory workers did not have to listen to Autonomen or Anarcho-syndicalists or independent workers who advocated strikes to prevent the government from putting in the missiles.

So when big rallies were scheduled for the fall, which the media had already labelled the "Hot Autumn", which could have ended up in shutting down cities or at least in large numbers of people being radicalized by radical speakers, the rules had changed. Political operatives from the Godfathers who worked in the Church, labor and mainstream party groups not only were in a majority in the planning meetings; some had infiltrated the real peace groups and sowed dissention in their ranks.

It was time to deal, and this was the deal: the churches, unions, and social democrats would get their people to the marches and rallies only if speakers agreed to address only the issue of the missiles and not connect that to other issues, and only if the only allowed position was that the people demanded that Parliament would vote to not accept the missiles. No direct action, no strikes, no civil disobedience.

The independent peace movement accepted the deal, though many of its members knew better. The majority did not really want to deal with a revolutionary situation; they favored, when the chips were down, gradual evolution by parliamentary decree.

They thought that with everyone in Germany against the missiles the government would vote against them. They thought that if the government betrayed them and voted for the missiles, then the people who were following the churches and unions and Social Democrats would again look to the independents for guidance.

Even the Green party leadership, at least enough of them, were bought off. They would vote against the missiles in Parliament with the Social Democrats, and when the majority Christian Democrats voted in the missiles anyway the Greens and Social Democrats would pick up votes in the next election, and the Greens would hold the balance of power. Of course, they would use it for ecology and all that, but in the meantime they would stop making calls for massive civil disobedience and making the country ungovernable.

All Jack's group, the anarchists, disillusioned Greens, and independent peace movement could do in the weeks leading up to the deployment of the missiles was try to explain what was happening to people in the hope that they would accept the need to disrupt the country once the Parliament had voted. Everyone was already against the missiles; the problem was that almost everyone had abnegated ultimate responsibility to Parliament. The press, of course, pretended that the outcome of the vote was in doubt, and the politicians did what they could to help promote that illusion. It would keep the country calm, and, hey, a close vote for the missiles would mean that the important next step was to elect more Greens and Social Democrats to the Parliament in the next election, so that they could get the missiles out.

Early in the morning of the day the vote was scheduled in Parliament anarchists and others started assembling in a park near downtown Bonn. Their stated purpose was to march to the Parliament and protest the vote. Of course the newspapers had announced that there would be thirty thousand police in town to prevent this. They began their preventive measures by waiting only until a few hundred people assembled in the park, and then hustling them out of the park. The protestors, not having an alternative plan, marched towards Parliament. The police hoped that by dividing up the protestors they could deal more easily with the smaller groups. The police were used to fighting the autonomen by then.

The autonomen were also used to fight the police. Most did not come to Bonn, feeling it was a trap, but those who did had not tried to gather at the park; they waited along the route and then joined the march when it reached them. Jack's group was towards the back of the march, which became several blocks long. Jack was supposed to try to get press coverage for the group, and used that excuse to take Tracy, his seventeen year old press aide, with him to the front of the march.

The march did not seem very impressive: a few hundred people trying to change the course of history. Almost all were less than 30 years old, many wore the leather preferred by anarchists and punks, all were dressed warmly for the winter weather. Mostly the crowd was silent, either determined or not quite sure what it hoped to do. The anarchists, anticipating that the police would not let people assemble in the park, joined the march as it walked along. Meanwhile Jack tried to follow their route on his map. They were far from the Parliament building when they found themselves marching between rows of green clad riot police. Most of the marchers were not intimidated: a single line of police is nothing to a massed crowd, not if the police aren't willing to shoot people.

Just before the head of the crowd reached the blocks near the parliament building that had been completely cordoned off by the police there were two spectacles. One was the head of the youth group of the Social Democrats, complete with speakers and sidekicks, exhorting the marchers to behave reasonably. The other was a line of women, a dozen or so of them, dressed in black robes like witches, wearing makeup so that they could not be identified, and carrying staffs. They beat their staffs on the ground in rhythm and the march approached. Then they stepped out into the street and became the head of the march.

The Strasse that was the police's line of defense was poorly chosen: it was quite wide, with plenty of room to maneuver, and traffic was already blocked off from it. The crowd followed the black witches to the right, along the continuous row of riot police. They walked a block, two blocks, three. Jack and Tracy began to wonder if the women were pacifists leading them away from their target.

In unison the line of black clothed women swivelled left and dashed into the police line, swinging their staffs; Jack and the rest paused a split second and charged after them. Most of the police were on the ground and the few that weren't grabbed individual people; the mob flowed around them. Jack had to turn back to rescue Tracy from a policeman, then they were running with the crowd down the street towards parliament. Looking back the policemen had reformed their line behind the crowd and were now keeping new people out. A hundred or so had gotten through.

They ran to the end of the block and smashed into another closed line of police. It was a melee now; the police were swinging their clubs, and some of the mob paused. One more line of police up ahead and then they would be able to turn left towards the Reichstag. But suddenly lots of reinforcements blocked the way; there is no way less than a hundred scattered and unpracticed people can punch through a police line four officers thick. The danger now was being arrested; more police were arriving by the second. The people's army reversed its direction and smashed back through the second police line, which now tried to pen them in. The police at the cordon line wisely decided to let the hundred or so people behind them back out into the main street.

The main crowd was now pressing against the police lines for a distance of about two blocks. The police brought up reinforcements for the shoving match. The crowd got larger and larger. The inevitable happened: the water cannons arrived. The massive green trucks lost no time: they started spraying the crowd with water. It was a cold enough day even without being wet. The crowd did not disperse. It tried to attack the cannons, and gangs of policemen had to form to protect them. This created a problem: it was hard for the water stream to hit the people without hitting the pigs.

It hit hard: it knocked people down. People wearing raincoats or leather for protection formed the troops to take on the police guarding the cannons. The others continued to press against the greenshirts guarding the Reichstag. The battle went on for an hour.

Within the chaos the crowd debated. They obviously were not going to get to the Parliament. There was no press coverage: the people of the world would see staid fools voting for nuclear war, not the battle in the streets. It was time to go mobile.

There were no leaders, no generals. Just people with some experiences in demonstrations talking to each other. At some point they reached a decision, collectively, voting with their feet: they began marching away from the masses of police and parliament. A rear guard remained, at first continuing to press up against the police lines, then gradually dispersing into the wide boulevard, milling about.

The demonstrators were heading towards downtown Bonn, carrying their banners and black flags. As soon as they were away from the polizei cans of spraypaint appeared and slogans were put on walls and parked cars. After a few blocks they reached the Embassy of El Salvador, which was protected by a total of three police. A few speeches were made and people began to spraypaint the building, then to break its windows. A police car was overturned and set on fire, then the building itself. It would not be on the evening news. Then again the people moved onward, now ecstatic, and starting to chant. They headed towards the university.

The police finally managed to get a line of cops across the street in front of the crowd, but the crowd just turned down another street. A few such maneuvers put them at the university, and the crowd grew larger. Students started blocking traffic by sitting in the streets. Soon traffic in Bonn was at a standstill.

Best of all, the police could not maneuver their cars and vans and water cannons; they had to pursue the demonstrators on foot. But whenever they managed to get a line of police together the crowd ran through it, not even having to hurt the police, just brushing them aside like so many lice.

Finally a large contingent of police got behind the crowd, but a bunch of little old ladies (no kidding, this really happened, no one knows who the ladies were) got between police and the demonstrators, and started walking very slow, refusing to let the police get past them. Soon the crowd had escaped again, but the collective wisdom was that it was time to disperse. By then it was a big party anyway: people had come out of their office buildings for lunch. The demonstrators mingled in small groups, talking. Most of the people whose cars were stuck in the jam were friendly: they understood about the missiles. It was a holiday, a party.

Chapter 8

LOVE

There were problems, to be sure, but on May 1st they seemed solvable. But risky: it was hard to be overly optimistic when he'd only been out of jail a few days and still had a trial ahead of him and the enemy had 60,000 nuclear weapons; but solvable.

There seemed to be a clear ordering of the problems: Blade, the RCP, the job, and the bourgeoisie. Blade and he had not made love for a month, and that in itself had to do with underlying problems. He had finally decided to act on the idea that the problems were hers as much as his: he was about to look for an apartment for himself.

Jack had met her two years earlier. He had already been talking to Belinda for a few months, and he had met with Blade several times when Belinda could not be available. He was even paying for the "Revolutionary Worker" by then: it made Belinda happy and did have well researched articles on what was going on in the world. There were a lot of things that he did not like about the RCP's ideology, but he thought they were open to discussion.

Blade was thin, a couple of inches shorter than Jack, and looked Japanese even though she was half Caucasian. She wore her black hair short with highlights of grey hair dyed purple-red. He could hardly look at her by then without being entranced. She seemed brilliant: she always had an explanation for political events, whether they were global in scope or a recent decision of some local amateur organization. Blade and Jack would sit in the bar, dark and homey, drinking mugs of cheap beer, discussing what had happened in the world and how to go about changing it. It looked like both The United States of America Government and The Union of Soviet Socialist Republics Government were going to get into a nuclear war one way or another. Blade and her RCP friends seemed to be about the only people in the world besides Jack who both realized that and had a serious plan to do something to prevent it. They had also provided Jack with intelligence reports on the various political grouping there were in Seattle. This had enabled Jack to stop wasting time trying to work with people who's real agenda precluded overthrowing the governments.

The day of the Peace fair it just so happened that Sandy and Jack were "broken up". In other words she was in her third attempt to get Jack to conform by saying she did not want to see Jack anymore, when she really did. But when it came to the bottom line, she was a liberal and a yuppie with an inheritance coming who was simply peace slumming, and was trying to pressure him into giving up the idea of armed insurrection and go for a safer option.

Since he was, as always, along with Sandy, a public representative of Nuclear Xchange, and the continuation of the newspaper as well as the relationship was in great doubt, there were serious openings in his defenses. Jack told Blade that he had broken up with Sandy. Yes, he was on the market for sale to the highest bidder.

Blade came to where he was sitting and told Jack about the ship. A West German cargo ship's crew had announced it would refuse to carry the Cruise Missile to Germany. The American news media had, of course, suppressed the story. The ship was in the harbor and some peace people had gone down there to greet the sailors. They had been turned back at the gate to the pier, and told that none of the sailors was leaving the ship.

Did he want to go down and try to get on the ship? We could interview the sailors and publish it in Nuclear Xchange. There were other people who might want to go. Did he think any of my friends would want to go?

It was a zoo, the Peace Fair. It was split between a dance marathon for Armistice and the Freeze over in the Food Bazaar and an auction for Physicians for Social Responsibility, a mini fleamarket for Nuclear Xchange, and a tabling area for the rest of the peace movement and assorted "progressives." Armistice was already thoroughly rotten and ready to disintegrate, the Freeze had been taken over by professional Democrat operatives whose task was to see that it died stillborn, and Nuclear Xchange had never been anything but the mascara on that old fart, government. People, well intentioned, wandered in and looked at the information booths, perhaps picking up a poster or a button, and then looked at the auction items and perhaps wrote down a bid, glanced at the fleamarket, and walked out again, having done a bit for peace. Jack spent occasional time trying to talk people into boycotting General Electric Company or joining in civil disobedience (he was his usual useless self as far as Nuclear Xchange went not bothering to help raise the money that would have helped catch up on the two months back pay he was owed), which was his volunteer effort.

No one he talked to considered going to the ship seriously, especially once they heard that it was Blade's, and hence the Revolutionary Communalist Party's, idea. Sandy, their illustrious editor and news hound, did not believe Jack: something like that would have been in the "Seattle Times." The Greenpeace people could not make decisions that quickly and suspected Blade. The rest of the peace movement wimped out: they were scared of any adventure that was not carefully planned and approved in advance by the people with the nuclear weapons.

Blade's recruits all fit in one car: the lawyer, Blade, Jack, Demetri, Sandy and Peggy. Demetri was a teenage member of the Revolutionary Communist Youth Brigade; he was of greek descent but spoke working class American without an accent. Peggy was a white woman with curly brown hair and acne; also a teenager. Sarah was a punk, medium size and stature, complete with short mohawk, studded leather jacket, and a limited command of the English Language. The lawyer drove us down to the docks. Jack had been along the waterfront before, but now we were in an area that had nothing but docks and warehouses. Huge cranes stood at the water at intervals move cargo to and from the ships.

They decided not to try to go in the gate first: that would tip off the guards that we were trying to break in. It was getting dusky. They drove along the road to where the section that the ship was docked at ended, then jumped out of the car, excepting the lawyer, who would pick them up at the end. There was a fence topped with barbed wire, three symbolic horizontal strands. No cars were in sight, and after some hesitation Demetri climbed over. One by one they did the same; it was not hard. Once on the other side they darted in among the trailers.

It was one of those containerized freight yards: most of the stuff was in trailers that would be moved around by semi's. They expected to be snatched up any moment like common thieves. The containers were in rows and they darted from one to another, closer and closer to the ship.

A piercing alarm went off. They stood in terror. No one seemed to be coming towards them, but they were ready to flee. After a minute of terror someone realized one of the giant cranes was moving; the warning signal was from it. They collected themselves and then moved on until they were as close to the ship's entryway as possible.

There was no guard protecting the ship itself. After a whispered conference they walked calmly across the open space to the gangplank. The dock workers ignored them. Moments later they were on the ship and went to look for the crew.

It was a big ship. They went through doors, up ladders, down ladders. They could find no one. They found ourselves outside again, on a sort of balcony, and guessed that the crew quarters would be towards the rear, then headed that way.

An enormous blond bearded sailor in a black uniform almost ran into them. Blade tried an introductory sentence in English. The sailor, said something, probably that he did not speak English, and went on his way.

The second sailor they found knew a few words of English, he was clearly German, and took us to the mate. The mate was a skinny, brown haired, bearded man who could easily have been a university professor if he had had the right clothes and been in the right place. His English was competent, if not polished. Yes, they had refused to carry the missiles. They had a lot of support in Germany. They were in some trouble, but it is not so easy to replace an entire crew. They were confined to the ship. Did we want to know something else? On their last voyage from Seattle they had loaded crates containing Boeing made Cruise Missiles.

"Are you sure?" Jack said "Boeing makes air launched cruise missiles. They aren't supposed to go to Germany. Germany gets only the ground launched cruise missiles."

"The crates were from Boeing. They were marked secret. The manifest said they were aerodynamic equipment, and they were being sent to the airforce in Germany. They were exactly the right size to carry an ALCM. We did not open the crates. What else could they be?"

"No wonder they won't let you off the ship. No wonder the newspapers did not bother to send reporters."

Blade gave them the "For a World Without Imperialism Contingent" flier. The mate was much more savvy than Blade was; he asked a few questions and figured out she was a leninist-maoist. He was not; the crew were against imperialism and nuclear weapons, but none of them were leninists and he personally thought that Bolshevism was a bad thing. If anything they were anarchist syndicalists. Blade would probably have argued all day but a buzzer went off and he said they had to cast off.

They walked out the front gate. The guard was pissed as hell but there was nothing he could do: the lawyer interposed himself and then drove them off.

Sandy, Jack's lover and editor of Nuclear Xchange, did not want to hear about it; anything involving the RCP was suspect. The Seattle Times had not covered it and there was no way to talk to the sailors to confirm the story. Jack thought it was mainly because he was on her shit list.

Jack called Blade and they agreed to get together to talk. They could meet at the donut shop. They walked over to Broadway from Jack's apartment, which was new only to Jack: it was spacious and swarming with roaches. Blade, to his surprise, asked if he wanted to go to her apartment. It was a tiny place not too far away. Despite the fact that he had an enormous crush on her he was not thinking this was romantic. She was always business, even if her business was radical politics. They talked about going to Germany for the Hot Autumn and about the ship. She explained away the RCP's lack of credibility by pointing out that the people in the peace movement were all middle class and essentially liberals. He was more concerned about the fact that the few anarchists they had persuaded to go to Germany decided to go on their own, not as part of the RCP contingent. She explained that they were individualists just looking for excitement, not disciplined enough to overthrow a government.

Before too long she complained that the apartment was too cramped. Since neither of them had much money they agreed to find a small park she knew about, and she suggested buying some beer to celebrate. He suggested wine instead and soon they had a cheap bottle and were wandering around the slope of Capital Hill facing the Sound, trying to find this little park. It took a while, but at last they found it. It consisted only of a few park benches with good views of the lit up downtown area, and the Sound beyond. They drank some wine and kept talking. It was getting chilly, like it always does in Seattle at night, even in the summer. She put her arm around his waste and he put down the bottle and they kissed. It was the sweetest kiss he had tasted in his life, an elixir of Blade's special smell and the tobacco she had just been smoking and his admiration for this fighting woman and the postcards his father had sent home from Japan when he was three years old and dad was in the occupying army, helping to fight the Korean War from a safe distance.

Soon they were walking back to the apartment. Blade had not been with a man for two years, and the dam had broken. They barely made it back to her apartment. Jack was totally entranced: her skin attracted his hands like none had ever done before, not even when he was a seventeen year old virgin, her face was the dark star of eternity, her body hot to the touch and totally alive. They delved into each other, electric sex currents flowing through their penis and vagina and up to their breasts and mouths, oscillating, resonating, exploding.

June first, slightly less than two years later, he moved into his own apartment, a studio on Second Avenue between downtown and the Space Needle. Blade and he had made love a couple of times after he announced he was moving out, but that was it. He had started sleeping in the living room, it was less frustrating. He was in deep trouble with the RCP, or they were in deep trouble with him: they said he was guilty of bad judgement and breaking party discipline. He was saying that the party needed to get its act together and their local leaders had shown bad judgement regarding the No Business As Usual anti-war campaign. He was seriously thinking that, if they were right about how close the US was to nuclear war, they should either be organizing a general strike or preparing to fight a Sendero Luminoso (Peruvian Communist Party) type civil war; the last thing they should be doing was doing whatever Baba Vakian told them, especially when that meant liquidating No Business As Usual except as a recruitment front.

The RCP believed in growth by purging: NBAU and the Party would grow if they forced out or alienated everyone who was foolish enough to disagree with them. They had grown from about 5000 members in 1972 to about 200 members by 1985 by this method, and by 1990 they would have grown to about 80 members.

RCP cell meetings started to be about him and his refusal to agree with the leadership and his insistence that the entire party debate certain questions after hearing his views. Finally he walked out of a cell meeting.

He found out the party was worried that he was influencing too many other people in and around the party with his arguments. Aside from his criticizing the bureaucracy judgment and lack of democracy within the party, they especially hated his criticizing The Single Party State, saying it was a capitalist institution and they should not be planning on setting up one if the government was overthrown.

By the time September rolled around he found himself sitting in a bar under the Space Needle having Slacmaster and Blade repeat to Jack his political errors and topping that with saying the party believed he was a police agent. He walked out. He never saw Blade again. He was under pressure to leave his job because they knew he was a communist and he had caught someone firing a woman because she was black. He decided Seattle was a waste of time and he would move to LA to regroup and organize around the Sendero's military strategy, but with a more tolerant attitude towards dissent. Also, he had started to read THE BOLSHEVIKS AND WORKERS CONTROL, which showed how the leninists subverted what was essentially an anarchist workers and peasant's revolution in Russia, and was considering whether vanguard parties really were inherently bourgeois in nature.

Jack was used to living at the poverty level, and he had saved a good sum of money, for him, once he stopped supporting Blade, so he figured it would be an easy move.

It usually does not snow in Seattle, but in November wave after wave of snow swept in. There was almost no snow removal equipment, the roads were dangerous, wrecks everywhere. He waited for the weather to do its usual trip and rain and wash the snow away. Instead it snowed more. He waited. It snowed more.

Masturbating is better than not having sex at all. How can you love someone else if you don't first learn to love yourself? Masturbation is better than a lot of things: food, work, sleep, most music. It is better than making love with someone you don't like.

It is healthy, it keeps the mind from building up unnecessary hatreds, fears, and tensions. Best of all, it is fantasy. In your imagination you can be anything and do it with anyone. You can imagine picking up a woman on the street and taking her home and balling her. You can imagine being a man and doing it with a man, or being a woman and doing it with a woman, or being a woman and doing it with another woman, which was Jack's favorite at the time. He knew that Blade secretly wanted to bed other women, and would not because it was against party rules, so he imagined he was her and doing it with the girls she liked, or one of those girls and doing it with Blade. Flirting, kissing, caressing, the excitement of nipples, the taste of vagina and having a tongue sweeping back and forth over his clit.

Jack had learned back in Berkeley, trying to imagine being a woman in order to write about women realistically. He would enter a state of self hypnosis and then make his body into a woman's body and then rub his tits until he had an orgasm. Later he learned to rub his penis and feel it as if it were being inserted in his vagina; when he ejaculated he had an orgasm as his imaginary male partner shot into his imaginary pussy. He began imagining being a woman, one ex-girl friend or another, and being with another woman and being seduced by her. He also tried to imagine what it was like being treated like a woman, being told the things girls are told from an early age, being placed in a clearly subservient class for no fault of your own.

Finally, in Seattle, it had not snowed for a few days and he had to vacate his apartment. Another snowstorm was on the way and he decided to drive south before it hit. Into the car with all of his possessions that would fit, leaving a TV and lots of other items for anyone who wanted them. Onto the freeway, south.

There was a chance of ice on the highway and snow was starting to fall. He was almost to Eugene and had decided he had better stop there. He was driving about 45 mph and most of the traffic was going about 50. A four wheel drive passed by rapidly to his left and slowly began to spin and drift over in front of him. He touched the brakes as lightly as he could and started to slide, drifting into the breakdown lane, watching the four wheel spin in front of him, turning his wheels in the direction of the slide, to no avail. There was no friction for the wheels to grip. He hit a metal post, grazing it, bouncing back into the highway, spinning the opposite way and a lot faster now. Other cars were sliding and spinning too.

The car stopped. It was facing 45 degrees back down the highway. Other cars, perhaps a dozen, were all stopped and pointed in different directions, but none had hit each other. The four wheel drive was on the opposite side of the road in the breakdown lane. He pressed in the clutch and turned the key.

A red car was trying to brake, trying to steer, trying to dodge the cars that were already stopped. It was moving fast and out of control. It avoided a dozen cars and aimed directly at Jack. Smash. His car went sliding across the icy asphalt like a marble.

He was not hurt. The car door beside Jack was totally smashed. The red sports car was pretty well smashed in one corner but was otherwise cool. A man asked Jack if he was O.K., then went away. It was very cold. A policeman showed up. The four wheel drive had driven away, unharmed and unquestioned. A tow truck arrived.

It would be at least two weeks before the car was fixed up. Jack flew to New York City. The cabby who picked Jack up at La Guardia was from Trinidad and told Jack about it. He was making it: his girl would go to college next year. $15 to get to Brooklyn, Park Slope.

Familiarity. Warmth. It was good to be back among friends. The brownstone house had not been turned into a middle class nightmare: Girard pled poverty when Brigid tried to redecorate. The stove in the kitchen had been dangerous and had been replaced, but the old round table was still there and people came and went, chatting with Brigid, drinking coffee, munching.

Sarah, Brigid's daughter, seventeen, was not much in evidence, and Brigid's son John was living with his father and visiting on weekends. Saul was three, becoming human. Robin, Brigid's sister, had moved in and was working a yup job in Manhattan. Tanya still lived there, had finished nursing school and was working at the Manhattan VA. Alice was an artist from LA. Danny, a tall blond jewish Brooklyn born professor, had just moved in. A merry crew. Sheila lived in a coop she had bought a few blocks away. None of his old girlfriends were around.

Early Winter. It was already dark, but with a sweater and a leather jacket Tanya was warm enough. Walking from the bus stop, already tired from the last shift and lack of sleep, moving mainly on the caffeine from a cup of coffee. Walking up the driveway of the great building, wishing her boyfriend would drop her off or at least pick her up, wishing she had a car.

Visitors were going in and out; it was a few minutes too early for the nurses to be coming off shift.

Glass doors side by side. Pushing through one set, then a second. The black bored face of the security guard smiled when he saw her and she smiled back, knowing nothing about him but having guessed in the past that he is over forty and married. Next there was the elevator. She was glad there were no doctors on it, just another nurse, no one she knows, moving a patient in a wheelchair. He was an old man. They were almost all old men in the VA hospital; this is not one of the warehouses where they keep the minions of cripples from Korea, Vietnam, and your everyday military operations accidents. Most of the undead from World War II had died; now it was just old men with weak hearts or swollen prostate glands or cancer or AIDS come in for treatment.

Intensive Care, ICU, cannot be taken in by the human brain all at once. Glancing in as Tanya did there was a stronger smell of antiseptic than out in the hallway, a symphony of synthesized machine sounds, and a tangle of machines and bodies. Things are alright; the nurses take in that a replacement has arrived without breaking their rhythms. Tanya turns into the locker room. Off comes the scarf of lavender wool swirls, followed quickly by the black cowskin jacket. Sitting on the bench she removes heavy boots and wool socks. Jeans slipped off reveal slender long legs, followed by shirt slipped off slender torso and arms. Her breasts are small and free for a moment, then the smock descends over her and she is sexless again, an angel.

Officially her shift has not begun but she looks at the patients as she chats with the Charlene,

Ramona, and Oni in turn. They are covering seven patients between them, five of them heart patients, one dying of cancer, one of general organ failure from years of drug abuse. By nature's way all of them would be dead.

The shift began with filling out forms. She would spend a lot of time on the shift trying to fill out the records and other bureaucratic forms in the hopes that when the shift was over she would not have to spend to much time finishing up her writing. In theory she should record every move she made, to make sure if the doctor's or hospital were sued their asses would be covered. In reality she had to keep the patients alive, which was contradictory to full record keeping.

She took two patients, Mulroney and Simmons, and both of them were asleep, more or less. Each had tubes leading into their bodies and tubes leading out; each had electrodes attached to their chests in the vicinity of the heart and a blood pressure monitor on one arm; Mulroney was tied with restraints since he insisted on pulling out the tubes that kept him alive whenever he woke up. One of the tubes went through his nose down into his single lung. Machines made soft beeping sounds beside each bed. Later she would have to change the sheets, but otherwise, with any luck, Tanya would have a quiet night.

"Hi Tanya." She was back from the evening shift. It was 1:30. Jack was in the kitchen with a notebook, trying to figure out how to make computers conscious.

"Hi Jack. Writing?."

"Just thinking, really. How was work?"

"Nothing unusual. Simmons and Mulroney tonight. Plus Hobbes, because Hillary's charge had a hypertensive crisis, but he's no problem, he shouldn't even be in intensive care, but if they sent him out to a ward he'd probably die from neglect. Simmons is barely hanging on, he's living on meds, and Mulroney is an asshole. He pulled his tubes out twice yesterday, we had to put him in restraints."

Once, at the end of some party, when he had been talking at length to her and she was a little drunk and stoned, years before, before he had gone to Seattle, she had felt soft for him, and had flirted, and been disappointed when he did not make a move on her. Most other times she had found him irritating, but he had changed in the years he was away. He had been just another fragile bizarre kid hoping to make the big time years ago: now he was solid, assured, able to take care of himself. She took care of other people enough already: she wanted someone to take care of her or at least not be a burden. And now he obviously liked her, whereas before he had been curious but distant.

She had talked to him for hours the first night he was back, and he really listened. Her boyfriend, Peter, had stopped listening years ago.

"Want to see what's on T.V.?" she said.

He got a slightly pained expression on his face, not liking TV, but then realized it was really a request for company, and looked pleased. He said O.K.

She sat on the Sofa between him and the T.V. She still felt fragile, the stress of nursing and feeling like she would never have a husband and child and mortality still eating at her heart, but she felt confident too, with this man who was lonely and good and who had no other woman. She restrained the urge to talk about Peter or her desire for a family. Neither of them was paying attention to the T.V.

"So what are your plans. Will you be here much longer?"

"They said it would be at least two weeks before the car is fixed. I'm going to try to get some temporary paralegal work so I'll be solvent when I get back out West. Of course, I was just going to Los Angeles to get away from Seattle and to be in, well, it is quite an experience to live there, I'll bet. You really are pretty. I like talking to you. It will be hard to leave."

"We haven't even slept together," she said.

"Isn't that odd? But you have Peter."

"Well." She said.

She was hoping he would take the initiative, put his hand on her, kiss her. It was weird. He seemed willing enough. She felt her pulse move a bit faster, her desire building, her breasts under her blouse. She moved her hand to his.

His eyes, blue eyes, were looking at her face, and without glancing at her hand, he moved his face closer.

They kissed, and it was like:

Pounds, Shillings, Dimes. Buying old heresies in nude bottles. Lips touch moist fallow sea muck. Hands lead arms to embrace pulsing. Insulation cotton/polyester lessening. Intensifying tongues of flame. Visions of disrobing. Television switched off, prick hard, pussy wet. They mount the stairs, creaking wood. Floor after floor, stepping. Skeletons interweaved muscles tensing. Relaxing beings pulsing eyes watching. Reflexing sensory nerves netting. The secret hearth reached, they embrace. A soft bed beneath a full moonlit window waits. Jack removes her shirt and she his pale torso strips. Phallicks waiting circumcised. She lies on her back and his big head lips puck. Tongues again, snakes in heat. He slides down her neck. Grasping her tit, jaguar pleasure spasm. His hands beneath her butt. Pleasure spasm ecstacy milk. His hands on her legs. Milk fountain fire tit. His mouth slides to the twin. She sits of the edge of the universe, giving birth to abyss behind and desire below. She is back in the room, flaking ceiling. Full moon over Park Slope. Smiling face descending into the unseen. Worm tongue parting the outermost gates. Sweet dream come true. Word shader beyond words. Sings of friction and the abyss. Sings of quantum and vastness. Sings of vacuum and the dance of life.

Warm mammalian birthright. She brings her hand to her own tits, old magick. Bubbles hidden in the wine. Bubbles hidden in the new bottle. Pressures singing out of time. Currents running tit to womb and tongue to head. Fragile liquid frozen bliss. Empty netting cast in empty ocean. Eyes rolling back into the head. She is dead. He smiles. She smiles back. Lying beside her, black star. Lying beside her, giver of life. She wants to so bad, to run hand along the beach of sand-time. Touch the lips, throat, breast, penis. Touch the legs, kiss the breast. Ring the penis, lick the breast. Desire curled chaos demanding. Thirst thirst thirst unquenched. Lovely feel of hot seal song. Lips moistened on bull semen song. Hand stroking ape krishna song. Tongue gasping demon seeding shlong. Sin sucking sex semen song. Witch transmuted. Nets recast. Inside out. She is the penis and the sucking. Friction pressure heat illusion. Fat frolicked cells a gluten. Sliding bathing nourished joy. Her penis crying love mouth pulling. Inside out and twice as long. Her mighty penis swelling pushing. Electric gliding heretic prong. Sings Lips around the phallic reeling. Sings hips the earth the oceans tongue. Sings Beyond the veils of human reason. The bio piston's sacred song. Behold the sweetness swelling under. Pulsing veins of seraphs blue. Fusion of the void colliding. Fusion of the lover's glue.

She came to her senses with the feeling of a babe satisfied, the semen salty pungent rolling down her throat, her hand sticky and her brain stretched with having come, having been his penis and the perfect pleasure of sucking at once.

She came to her senses with the feeling of a babe satisfied, the semen salty pungent rolling down her throat, her hand sticky and her brain stretched with having come, having been his penis and the perfect pleasure of sucking at once. Then she slept.

It only took a couple of months for the ecstacy to corrode in the reality of the city. There was no talking to him. Tanya had made up her mind. He was a Stalinist Palestinian lover who would never allow her children to go to Synagogue school. He also was never going to make enough money to be a good father, was unstable, and a lousy writer. She had other men who wanted to go out with her, including her old boyfriend who was a musician and very funny and also Jewish.

So there was Tanya, gazelle body lying not ten yards down the hall from him, and there was Jack, reduced to beating off. Fortunately he had other things to do, politics and general prankstering, and with a job to boot he only let his emotions turn sad with longing for her on occasion.

There were lots of nice women to talk to, to look over, to consider the weight of entanglement versus its pleasures. There was his goddess Sheila, beautifully dark woman carrying Asian features via Eastern Europe and Philadelphia, but she was deeply involved with some Gurjief freak at that point. Brigid had a number of friends, most of them married, all of them intelligent and attractive. Dianne had a large graceful body, becoming voice and the blue eyes of the white mutant race, but she lived far away. Candy, Brigid's sister, was a bright, professional, warm slavic beauty radiant in her lack of pretense. Melissa was an ex-radical (don't say that to her, she feels guilty) with her own business and a coop apartment in a restored brownstone where a few years before only poor Haitians and transplanted blacks from the south lived. But each woman had her drawbacks, from his point of view, so he preferred to just dream about them, pull on his own penis, and remain friendly.

Then there was Linda. She was the most beautiful white woman he had ever seen. The first time he had walked into the kitchen and she had been sitting there, talking to Brigid, his mind had flashed warnings up from the depths that when he recovered were glossed with phrases: "she's got a boyfriend," "she must be married," "so what."

She smiled and paid attention to Brigid, who got up, hugged Jack, introduced him, and went back to talking about the latest exploits of her three year old, Saul, who moments later ran into the room tagged by a girl obviously smaller and younger and soon discovered to be Linda's daughter. Safe, Jack told himself, and now allowed himself to look a bit more at Linda, trying to see what made her so beautiful.

Her hair was almost black, but like an Irishwoman's, not like asians or blacks. Her skin was light and her face a well proportioned oblong. Her lips were full without lipstick.

The following days and weeks he tried not to think about her and, unlike with other women he met, did not imagine having sex with her. He had learned from Brigid that she was separated from her husband and that her child was very, very sick and had been born with internal defects.

She came by the house on occasion, usually with Lila, her child, and Jack would talk to her when he could. It was just part of the ongoing tea party that Brigid managed almost daily, cups of coffee and tea and gossip drunk by a moving cast of characters who were often there even if the queen herself were absent. Linda was studying to be a nurse; she had dropped out of college. This meant she was very friendly to Tanya, who had just finished nursing school, and Jack and Tanya had not yet broken up.

After a few of weeks of being tortured by Tanya's refusals Jack called up Linda and asked her out. She said she had exams coming up in school, but she could get together with him when they were over. A week and a half.

Her apartment was in a yuppie building being reclaimed in what was still a rundown section of Park Slope. It was spacious by Jack's New York Standards. The floor was polished wood, some walls were exposed brick, and the high ceiling was supported by wooden beams. She explained that the building had been a clock factory, and that her father was paying for the apartment.

Conversation tapered off rapidly after that. They tried kissing. It was hard to put their bodies close together, sitting on the sofa. Linda led the way to the bedroom. They became a bit shy, pausing, wondering whether to embrace in bed and then take off their clothes. Without speaking they removed their clothes first. Their bodies were as well proportioned as their faces, touching each other Gently as they rolled into bed. Over a year, and before that Jose's penis was as much punishment as his fists and his coke and his rage. Jack is different, even shrouded in a condom, far different, why he likes Linda, she doesn't know, but her breasts are heavy and her juices are flowing, were flowing even back on the sofa, and he lies on his back connected to her with a tongue emanating life gently and his penis good and hard and his hands moving over her gently so that as soon as he touches her breasts she cannot wait and lifts her hips, reaches back for his penis and shoves it up into herself, and her clitoris is so sensitive just the mild stimulation of her rocking hips drives her slowly to madness, looking at his face, his torso, his hands firing her tits, strings of hot flesh running through her body, rocking, moaning, harder, faster, his face now surprised, losing control, rocking, the orgasm creeping up, building up, body rocking, breasts burning, muscles twitching, pressure building, pleasure an intense jag, exploding.

Later there was Jim, an anarchist queer fairy from out of town. An experiment: Jack was not sexually attracted, but had imagined sucking on a penis often enough to want to try it in reality, and Jim seemed like a good, easy going man to do it with. They had on unlubricated rubbers, just over the tips of their penises, neither of them having any desire to be infected with HIV. It was fun, fingering the penis, kissing it, hearing Jim grunt with pleasure, licking it down, wrapping his fingers around it and squeezing down hard even as his own penis was throbbing (one thing about gay men, everyone said, is that they know how to suck a man off, which many women seem to have trouble with; but then lesbians say most men can't give good head to women), taking it in his mouth, slipping inside his lips, along his tongue, down into the throat, until they were in rhythm, floating in an ocean of pleasure, wave after wave, and finally jerking into each other.

Jim was gone the next day, and a few days later Jack was in love again, with a woman from where he worked. But he finally felt emotionally as he had believed mentally for years: he could love a woman and, in the course of things, still be left by her or leave her: the only eternal vow worth making was to the truth, and no one human embodied that. People still existed, just as the world existed, when they were away from you: to demand that someone be always with you is to deny their reality.

First in each human's life there was mother, nature, the Goddess, and the womb; her divinity is questioned only by fools. On earth many remember her with their bodies, though their minds and spirits are hurt by the sickness of power, patriarchy, and the evil books, the Bible, Vedas, and the Koran. To know and love the Goddess, mother earth, mother universe, in whatever form she takes, is the only true spirituality. The universe is a whole, and men and women are lucky that love is part of their lot.

LES GIRLS

"Big deal. Another boy ego. What a jerk."

"At least he tried. He might still learn."

"He's not trying to learn what it's like to be a woman. He's jerking himself off. He likes pretending he has tits and a clit and a vagina. Does he pretend he gets a period once a month? No Way."

"Well, at least it makes him a better lover. Which is a pain in its own way. Like an expensive drug."

"Really, though, let him imagine being brought up to cook, raise children, and be a handmaiden to some male jerk who can't distinguish between love and an occasional orgasm. Let him imagine being put in a institution for leaving home and becoming a poet and defying his father."

"It's possible, you know. He could imagine it, if he wanted to. I think in a way he knows, he knows how awful things can be and that he has had some privileges being a male. Just like we've had some privileges being white and educated, but we are pretty sensitive to what happens to colored women."

"I guess you're right. But the concentrating on sex stuff is pretty upsetting. It's not much different than men looking at pornography about lesbians, thinking how much fun it would be, never willing to admit that they might not mind being a girl for a day if they were a lesbian and could keep all their other privileges."

"Well, there's only one thing worse than having your period. That's work. Five days a week, hell I'd take two periods a month to get out of those five days a week. Useless work, destructive work. It's the main thing that unites us, the common mark of slavery."

"Well, true enough. Jack works like the rest of us. When he absolutely has to."

Laughter all around.

Chapter 9

ANARCHY

When the assembly of the people met for the second time no one tried to stop them. They met in the meadow by Holler's stream in the late afternoon. Sheriff Wilson and all the deputies came, but they had resigned themselves to being ordinary people for a while.

There were roughly five hundred people living in their community. The nearest town, Easting, twelve miles away, had a meeting scheduled for the following day, although the forces of authority thought they were still in control there. There were about three thousand people living in and around Easting.

They had declared their independence from Easting at the same time they had declared their independence from Oregon and the United States of America. Their community didn't have an official name, they had always told people they "lived up the valley east of Easting" or "Below Owl Ridge east of Easting." There was no town, just a general store and gas station. Everyone else was scattered about in houses, cabins, trailers and even huts, tepees, and tents.

A few families had been there as early as the end of the nineteenth century, small farmers and loggers. Many had come in the late 1960's and early 1970's, hippies determined to leave the big cities behind and get back to nature. More had come in the late 1980's and early 1990's, Earth First! people and anarchists and more refugees from the cities. A recent influx of friends of the old timers who had realized that with the eco-crisis disrupting food supplies and the industrialists and government determined to use force to hold onto power, survival might be largely a matter of living in a rural area, completed the crew.

Everyone knew just about everyone, and there had been plenty of talk about what needed to be done since the last assembly. A lottery was prepared in advance and Cedar (formerly Betty Polowski) and Lucy White won the draw to facilitate. They consulted briefly, then got everyone quiet.

"As far as we know, everything's been pretty much talked out and there's about as much consensus as we can get given how many of us there are. However, if anyone want to make a speech, or a comment, or offer something for resolution that Cedar and I don't know about yet, speak up now. Or whenever. Anyone want to speak before Lucy says the resolutions?"

No one spoke up, not even the dozen or so Loyal Americans in the crowd.

"O.K., here are the resolutions." Lucy White was a tall, black woman who liked to dye her hair red. "I'll read all of them and then we can go back and vote on them. First, we affirm our autonomy and independence from all governments and authority. Second, we are willing to cooperate with any autonomous group or individual in projects of mutual aid. Third, we will protect the environment in this area, including lands that the timber company and government and others claim to own, as we see fit. Fourth, any disputes between individuals that they cannot be worked out between themselves or mediated by a friend will be taken up by this assembly of the people. Fifth, that as far as sending delegates to larger assemblies, anyone can go and watch, but our voting positions will be evenly divided between delegates elected by lot and delegates elected by ballot. And sixth and last, anyone sent here to assert any authority over us will be arrested by a people's posse and forced to leave. Now I'm going to go over these things one at a time."

Robert Fowler, the store owner, said that maybe they should not bother to declare their independence again, because they could be independent just fine if the government fell, but if the central government was able to maintain order then they might be tried for treason later. But people had already talked that out: they knew they were independent, they made the resolution in order to encourage other people to become independent. The vote was roughly eighteen against, everyone else for.

When the resolutions were over and adopted the real debate began again, informally. It had two components: whether to limit the population of their community in order to protect the ecosystem, and whether to do traditional organic farming or the new wild farming system.

Jack and Mary were in favor or the wild system and of allowing new people into the community. Ann and Simon were old style organic farmers and wanted to stop people from coming in.

"We couldn't possibly raise enough wild food on our land to sustain us," said Ann. "Also, I think organic farming minimizes damages to the environment. At least we have all of our domesticated crops in one place, and that leaves more room for true wilderness. If we let more people in they'll have to farm and eat up more land, and like you say yourself we need excess capacity, not to strain the limits of the land."

Mary waited a moment before replying. "But now we have lots of land. It doesn't belong to the timber companies and government any more. To do organic farming on it we'd still have to cut down trees. With wild farming we just scatter seeds and see what grows. It requires less labor because we don't have to weed or kill insects. You know the ozone layer is going, and that means that the more diverse our food supply is, the more likely we are to survive."

"We're more likely to survive if there's enough to eat. A quarter acre organic garden can easily feed a family of four. We won't have to spend all our time wandering through the woods."

"Why can't we do both?" said Simon.

"Of course most people will do both," said Mary. "But there is one other consideration. A garden can be easily wiped out, from the ground or with Agent orange. Concentrated food supplies could make us a target for the government's soldiers or urban mobs."

"Things will settle down. They aren't going to treat us like the Vietnamese."

"Why not? We're their enemies now. A threat to their rich and powerful existence."

"That's why we still need to welcome good people in," said George. "The more good people we have, the better chance we have of defending ourselves and the earth. The future looks difficult, I hate to be a pessimist, but a lot of our people are going to die. That's what I think."

"He's right," said Jack. "If we take some people now, and things aren't as disastrous as we think, they can always move along later. But when the government can't deliver food to the cities there are going to be mobs heading out into the country, and right wing survivalist come lately's, and soldiers to collect food for themselves and the rich and the bureaucrats. I still think that while our main strategy against soldiers has to be to retreat into the mountains, that we should be buying more rifles and learning to use bows and arrows."

"Well, there I'll agree with you," said Ann. "We should also set things up to cut off the roads."

The discussions went on. There was the question of what to do if one of the other autonomous communities were attacked by the army, police, or right wing militia. Mostly it was felt that the only reasonable response to a large show of force was temporary compliance or retreat, followed by sabotage and guerilla warfare. At present, however, the forces of authority were having too hard of a time keeping order in the cities to bother with sending troops to rural areas.

That night three of the local affinity groups met for what would be their largest concerted effort to date. Despite the growing economic depression and chaos MegaCorp was still clearcutting forests on their "private property" in the area. This was despite the fact that the two highest ranking officers in MegaCorp had been killed lately by the bands of assassins that were after the country's tyrants and despoilers. Because sabotage of timbering equipment had become so widespread in the Pacific Northwest a group of about a dozen security guards – essentially a well armed militia – were stationed to protect the bulldozers, trucks and other equipment of destruction.

Security was the country's only growth industry, so it had been easy to get two of their unemployed sympathizers jobs on the night shift. Tonight they would be in a position to turn off the elaborate alarm system.

They went in groups of three to five for about fifteen miles on bikes, hiding off the road when any car came by. About a mile before the first security checkpoint they went off on a side trail. They still had three rough miles to go before reaching the equipment area.

According to plan they carefully deployed around the site. Sharpshooters took up positions in case there were surprise corporate reinforcements from the logging road. Their friends gave the signal that the security alarms had been turned off.

Jack pointed his handgun at a security guard's head and whispered "freeze." In a moment they had the man's weapon and walkie talkie, then tied him to a tree and gagged him. Around the equipment encampment the same scenario occurred a handful of times, including with their friends, and then they were free to work on the equipment.

"I'm glad the bear clan knocked out that tractor factory," said Mary. "They won't be able to replace these suckers anytime soon."

The security equipment was quickly trashed, the communications equipment placed with the captured weapons to be taken and stashed in the mountains. They hauled wood and placed it under the tractors, trucks, and mobile winches. Everyone except two people and the sharpshooters set off back down their trail. After they had been given a fifteen minute start the remaining saboteurs doused the wood with diesel fuel and then ignited their bonfires.

Then they fled. With ten or twenty million dollars worth of equipment going up in smoke, exploding as the fuel tanks reached their flash points, MegaCorp was not likely to come back to this area with logging equipment anytime soon.

Chapter 9

THE FUTURE

Jack's eyes were still lively in a calm way. His face was furrowed like plowed land but was mostly hidden by his long white beard and hair.

The people had gathered around, almost forty of them; everyone was there because he had announced earlier it would be his last talk.

"You know that I'm going to say nothing new. You know my body is old and falling apart inside, and that this is my last talk. You've all been good to me, and I thank you for that."

"This used to be a state called Oregon, and it used to be in the United States of America. We came here in the 1990's, about fifty years ago, because we knew the earth was being killed. We came because we wanted to live as full lives as we could and maybe to help save the earth from the people who were killing it. But it was already too late."

"We should have blown up the factories before we came here, the CFC factories if nothing else, but we didn't. By the time we realized the danger the government and the industrialists had agreed that the factories would be closed down in a few years. It would have been dangerous, and probably we would have got ourselves killed for nothing. The CFC's were already eating up the ozone layer then. But we should have done it, because if we had done it the ozone might have started coming back five years or a decade earlier."

"We think the ozone layer is coming back now, but we can't be sure, and it will be a slow process. It may be decades before we can extend the farm areas and longer before the wastelands start to come back of their own accord. As far as we know we are the only living enclave; every human, every animal save some insects, and every plant except some fungi and some annuals is dead, except maybe what lives at the bottom of the ocean."

"When we came here it was still like paradise, with great forests and immense farms spreading out hundreds of miles. The ozone was just beginning to thin and only a few of the most sensitive plant and animal species were getting sick and dying. We came here because the land was cheap, there weren't many people, and it rains a lot. We were lucky."

"We were here two decades before the panic really hit in the United States. It had bought food grown in poorer countries while the people in those countries starved. The government and the industrialists crushed two attempted revolutions here and killed millions of people. We survived because their system of control was disintegrating and we hid in the hills until they stopped watching our farm."

"There were lots of other people like us in this region, and in many ways we have been lucky to survive. The great trees died but their shade allowed plants to grow at their feet. The rains kept the dead trees from burning like they did in most places when drought came. We cut a wide swath of dead trees down around our lands in order to prevent the great fires from taking our trees, and we have the river water to keep us alive and save our trees from fire when they are dry.

"The world just kept falling apart. The industrialists tried feeding people with food grown from petroleum, and they built underground cities and special greenhouses that kept the ultraviolet out so that the rich people could eat vegetables and even meat instead of petro food. Nations fought each other over food supplies and over petroleum. Every year there were fewer people. We had better radios then, we kept track of what was going on. Things fell apart to the point where they could no longer maintain their greenhouses and petroleum factories."

"In the U.S. the desert expanded. First the great plains turned into a dustbowl, then the midwest, and finally even the east coast. The industrialists bred plants that were supposed to be able to take the ultraviolet, but it never really worked. The rest of the world was the same way, every year the dead zones grew. Whole cities of people died of starvation.

"Eventually the industrialists clustered around the oil producing regions, but their technology could not make up for their inner sickness. Sometimes their slaves revolted and tore everything apart. Other times they simply could not keep their equipment repaired. A few cases of mass suicide occurred, where people just deserted the cities and wandered out in the deserts to die.

"One by one the radio signals died. We weren't doing so well here either. Plants we had been able to grown for a while began to die as the radiation got more intense. But we cooperated with each other, and with the other enclaves in the region that were left. We got some UV glass from the dead industrial city, Portland, you've all heard that story many times, and we set up our greenhouses. We did not go crazy, we lived as best we could, we witnessed what happened and have passed knowledge from generation to generation. When other enclaves failed the people were welcome here. But even with the births there are less of us alive now than when we started.

"Five years ago the last radio signal stopped. It was from Southeast Asia, in a tongue we don't understand, so we don't know what happened. Maybe there are other people out there alive, maybe like us they don't sent out radio signals for fear of being raided. Maybe it is time we sent out a radio signal; there doesn't seem to be much danger any more. That's for you to decide together.

"Our Dobson station tells us that the UV levelled out during the last decade and it seems like it may be starting to decline. That means life will come back. It means we will see if our way of life is a good one. Genetically we should be ok, we are probably the most diverse species on earth at this point. Every race runs in our blood, and even though there are only a few people in each generation we haven't seen any bad effects of inbreeding yet.

"We should have destroyed those factories. I should have done it myself, because even if it had killed me it might have saved you, the world would be a little more alive now. I can't change the past.

"I am going to die soon, and that will mean there is room for another child. That makes me happy.

"We should have destroyed those factories, but the funny thing is that lesson will be lost. The factories will be dust soon, and the word will have no meaning. It will be centuries before anyone thinks to build a factory, maybe even millennia, and our little bit of wisdom will be forgotten.

"I guess that is all. I hope the earth is fruitful again, and that many of you live to see it that way."

After dinner Jack returned to his quarters. No one bothered him. He looked through his memorabilia, remembering people, places and times long dead. Then he lay down, but he did not sleep. Like many old people he did not sleep much. When all were asleep he got up again. He had repaired his pack and his clothes. He left no note.

He left the quarter and started up the river path. The moon was full and the sky was without clouds; he had counted on this. The path ended where the great trees ended, and he had to walk carefully to avoid falling on the rough ground. He soon was past the clearing and in the charcoal grounds. Moths flew around him, and he was glad that something could live still on the roots of trees long dead. He moved steadily on, slow paced but not stopping to rest.

When the sun came up he did not look for shade. It was not likely that anyone would follow him, but he wanted to be sure. He put on his protective hat and goggles and made sure not the tiniest bit of skin was exposed. When the sun was high in the sky he was beginning to bake and found a boulder near the river that offered shade.

Before the sun set he started off again. Occasionally he had to ford a stream that cut across the barren land. As he went he noted that fungi that had burst up in the night and burned in the day. Before the night was over he came to a major tributary of the river. He was determined to stay on the main river, but had to walk miles up the tributary before he found an old bridge that allowed him to cross.

Sometimes there were ancient roads along the river that made the going easier. He was already in the foothills and could see the mountain peaks. When he came to where two tributaries met he always followed the larger one, but already it was more of a rapidly moving stream that a river.

In the mountains the stream ran even faster, and he made progress slowly, stopping to rest frequently as he made his way up the hill. He spent as much time following the stream into the mountains as he had spent walking along the lowlands.

At last he found the place where the spring came out of the ground. He made his camp there and rested for a day, eating what little remained of the food he had brought.

He thought about many things, of the stars he had hoped to explore as a child, of the wars he had seen and read about, of mankind's history and religion and science. He thought about his lovers and their children. He thought about his body, thinking about how each part worked, warning it that it was about to die. He thought of the billions of years of life's evolution and how it had been destroyed by a chemical thought to be harmless to life. And he chided himself for not telling the family the truth: that he had figured that even if they destroyed the CFC factories back in 1989 the earth would have still died. Mankind was a diseased species, bent on destroying itself. If it wasn't the CFC's destroying the ozone layer it would have been something else, nuclear war or some industrial by product or just plane paving over the living earth.

When he could judge by the moon that the sun was on the opposite side of the earth from him, he lay beside the stream, gashed his wrist deeply with his razor, made sure he had cut the artery, and put his arm into the cold spring water.

The cold seeped into his body and he watched the stars. Time slowed down and he felt the parts of his body dying one by one. But the stars did not go away. He knew them and he knew the earth under him, and he drifted up, spreading out, seeing more and more. He saw the great continent and then the two great oceans, and where the earth divided the light from the dark. He drifted to where the sun's energy created ozone, and he saw the brown continents and dark oceans below him, and circled the earth, and filtered the sun.

Also from III Publishing:

THE LAST DAYS OF CHRIST THE VAMPIRE

by J.G. Eccarius

He rose from the dead . . .

His power grew over the ages. Enslaving minds and bodies through religious hierarchies and direct telepathic control, Jesus Christ promised people eternal life in return for obedience.

Professor Holbach thinks Christ the Vampire is just a metaphor giving him nightmares. But when he starts telling his story to others he and his friends are attacked and must flee for their lives. This is the story of how they fight back against this ancient horror.

Read the Book. Soon you'll see the graffiti. Then you'll live the reality . . .

"One of the most wildly blasphemous books we have seen since the classics of sacrilege."

– Fifth Estate

"A book of stunning originality, full of surrealistic shocks and haunting images."
– Robert Anton Wilson

"Iconoclasm at its most engaging ... be forewarned, you'll never want to take holy communion again!"

– Eva Von Kesselhausen

"Takes the vampire theme for a ride on a new roller coaster ... fun, entertaining, and in a few places hilarious."
– L. Chernyi in **Anarchy**

THE LAST DAYS OF CHRIST THE VAMPIRE, paperback, $6.00 from
III Publishing

Also Available:

@ SAMPLES by various people. Includes Codicioso (Greed), Thoughts on Anarchist Community Defense, and Anarcho Syndicalism and the Eco-Crisis. Pamphlet, 40 pages, $2.00.

Please add $1 for postage and handling.

Spread the word! Order 4 or more copies of THE LAST DAYS OF CHRIST THE VAMPIRE and take a 20% discount off the cover price.

III Publishing, P.O. Box 620362, San Diego, CA 92162

Some Alternative Information Sources:

MAGAZINES

FACTSHEET FIVE, Mike Gunderloy, 6 Arizona Avenue, Rensselaer, NY 12144-4502. Single issue $3.00. Six issue subscription $16. Every two months this reviews, briefly, all of the small press and underground magazines, books, recordings and miscellany that they find out about. A tremendous resource. Everything from the ultra-right to the ultra-left to ultra-sex to comics, the incomprehensibly esoteric, and the just plain weird. A good starting point for freeing yourself from the U.S. propaganda machine and for making new friends.

IDEAS AND ACTION, P.O. Box 40400, San Francisco, CA 94140. Single issue $2.00, four issue subscription $7.50. The magazine for people who are serious about working class people creating an anarchist society without bosses or bureaucrats. Put out two or three times a year by Workers Solidarity Alliance, the U.S. section of the International Workers Association, the anarchist international. News, analysis and occasional satire.

ANARCHY, c/o C.A.L., P.O. Box 1446, Columbia, MO 65205-1446. Single issue $2.00, six issue subscription $8.00. Every two months Anarchy brings you alternative news, reviews, lists of contacts, and essays that explore the limits of authority and autonomy in our world. Topics include sexuality, ecology, and of course, anarchy. Lots of great graphics.

FIFTH ESTATE, P.O. Box 02548, Detroit, MI 48202. Single issue, $2.00, three issue subscription, $5.00. The longest running underground newspaper in the U.S. that we know of, it consistently challenges the preconceptions people have about the nature of our civilization. Always interesting.

EARTH FIRST! P.O. Box 7, Canton, NY 13617. Single issues are $3.00, one year's subscription is $20. Truly radical environmental journal. For those who prefer to save the environment rather than just talking about it or praying to slimeball politicians. No Compromise in the Defense of Mother Earth!

INDUSTRIAL WORKER, IW Collective, 400 W. Washington #2B, Ann Arbor, MI 48103. $2.00 for 6 month subscription. Put out by the Wobblies, (Industrial Workers of the World) America's oldest radical union, still young and still upsetting bosses. Organizes inside and outside of traditional areas, for instance with environmental workers, child care workers, prisoners, and prostitutes.

LIVE WILD OR DIE, no address, moves every issue, try Fact Sheet Five or your local Earth First! group for a current address. "After the Deluge, Hastening the downfall, hearkening the dawn." Seriously sabotaging the industrial mindset, combining the environmental stance of Earth First! with a concern for social issues.

HOMOCORE, c/o World Power Systems, P.O. Box 77731, San Francisco, CA 94107. Send $1.00 cash only. "Fuck Sexual Conformity". Whether you are hetero or gay or off the scale.

PROCESSED WORLD, 41 Sutter St. #1829, San Francisco, CA 94104. Single issue $3.50. Consistently funny satire and social commentary, often about office workers, computer programmers, etc. Learn about how Amerika runs from people who see it as peons working in the centers of power and greed.

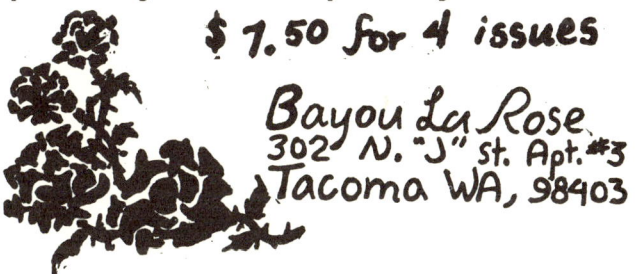

$7.50 for 4 issues

Bayou La Rose
302 N. "J" St. Apt. #3
Tacoma WA, 98403

BOOKS (mail order):

LEFT BANK DISTRIBUTION, 4142 Brooklyn N.E., Seattle, WA 98105. A complete catalog of anarchist literature.

AMOK, 859 N. Virgil, Los Angeles, CA 90029. Have you ever wondered if maybe, somewhere, a few men are controlling everything going on in the world? A catalog of paranoia, conspiracy theory, truth posing as fiction, and good unclean fun.

LOOMPANICS, P.O. Box 1197, Port Townsend, WA 98368. A catalog appealing to individualist and right wing anarchists, with useful information for all: weapons, tactics, finances, technology, fake i.d. and tax avoidance, and lots more.

MUSIC

Support your local live musicians! If there are only zombies in your neighborhood, try BLACKLIST MAILORDER, 181 Shipley St., San Francisco, CA 94107, or FACTSHEET FIVE.

TELEVISION

Smash it. Better yet, find a tall building and drop it on an executive. There's no such thing as good TV.